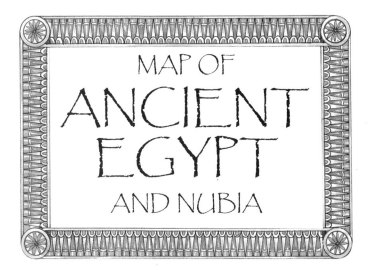

MAP OF
ANCIENT
EGYPT
AND NUBIA

MAIN SIGHTS

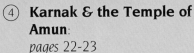
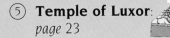

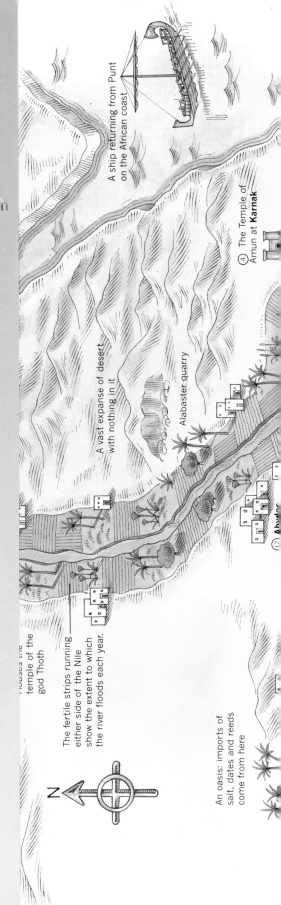

A ship returning from Punt on the African coast

④ The Temple of Amun at **Karnak**

A vast expanse of desert with nothing in it

Alabaster quarry

The fertile strips running either side of the Nile show the extent to which the river floods each year.

...temple of the god Thoth

An oasis: imports of salt, dates and reeds come from here

N

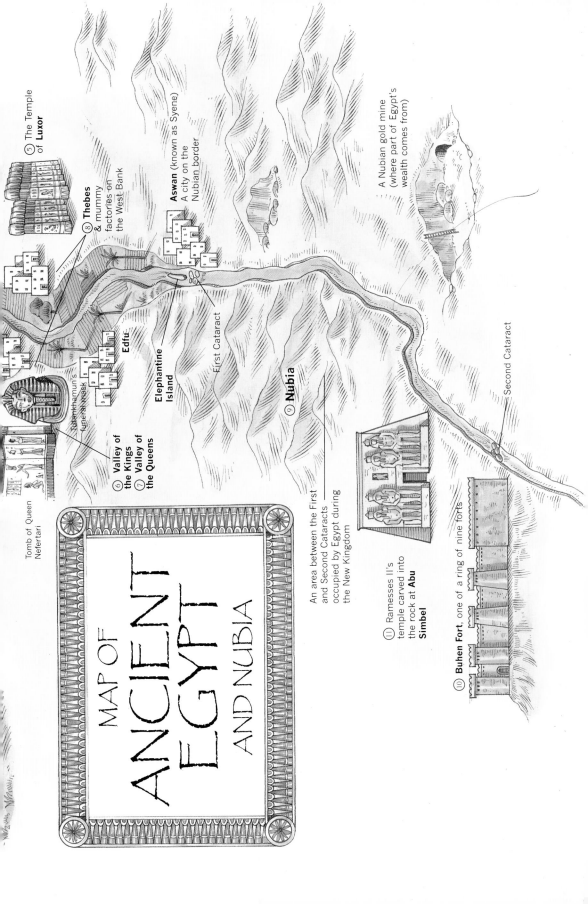

⑤ The Temple of **Luxor**

⑧ **Thebes** & mummy factories on the West Bank

Aswan (known as Syene) A city on the Nubian border

A Nubian gold mine (where part of Egypt's wealth comes from)

Tomb of Queen Nefertari

Tutankhamun's funeral mask

⑥ **Valley of the Kings**
⑦ **Valley of the Queens**

Edfu

Elephantine Island

First Cataract

⑨ **Nubia**

Second Cataract

MAP OF ANCIENT EGYPT AND NUBIA

An area between the First and Second Cataracts occupied by Egypt during the New Kingdom

⑪ Ramesses II's temple carved into the rock at **Abu Simbel**

⑩ **Buhen Fort**, one of a ring of nine forts

A VISITOR'S GUIDE TO ANCIENT EGYPT

Lesley Sims

Illustrated by Emma Dodd,
Ian Jackson & John Woodcock

Designed by Lucy Parris
Edited by Jane Chisholm
Managing Designer: Mary Cartwright

History consultant: Dr Anne Millard

First published in 2000 by Usborne Publishing Limited,
83-85 Saffron Hill, London EC1N 8RT, England.
Copyright © 2000 Usborne Publishing Limited.
The name Usborne and the device 🎈 are
Trade Marks of Usborne Publishing Limited.
First published in America in 2001

U.E. Printed in Spain

www.usborne.com

 # CONTENTS

EGYPT & THIS GUIDE

This book is a guide to what you'd find if you could visit Ancient Egypt in the reign of Ramesses II, also known as Ramesses the Great – especially to himself. Ramesses II was pharaoh, or king, of Egypt from c. (about) 1289 to 1224BC.

Ramesses II on his throne. His official title is "King of Upper and Lower Egypt", dating back to the days when Egypt was two separate kingdoms.

A BRIEF HISTORY

The beginnings of Egyptian civilization can be traced back to about 5000BC (Before Christ was born). For convenience, historians split Egyptian history into periods (see pages 62-63). Ramesses II ruled during one of the most important: the New Kingdom.

Originally, Egypt was simply a collection of villages along the banks of the Nile, the river running from north to south on the eastern side of North Africa. By 3200BC, the villages had merged, forming two independent kingdoms. Called Upper and Lower Egypt, each fought to control the other.

A slate carving of an Upper Egyptian king executing a prince from Lower Egypt

Then, in about 3100BC, Menes, a king of Upper Egypt, conquered Lower Egypt, and united the kingdoms. Menes founded a capital at Memphis and his family became the first of 31 dynasties (ruling families) to govern Egypt.

WHAT'S IN A NAME?

Don't be confused if you come across different spellings of Ramesses. Modern spellings vary, because the Ancient Egyptian form of writing, *hieroglyphics*, can be translated in different ways. Ramses and Rameses are also sometimes used – but they're all the same king.

A RIVER CRUISE

One of the best ways to see Egypt is from the river. You can travel the length of the country, from the Mediterranean to the edge of the Nubian desert. Turn to pages 16-40 to see the sights in the order you'd visit them if you set off from the Nile Delta. Ramesses II is currently building a new capital city for himself at **Per Ramesses** (see map on the right). It's a good starting point for a trip as many boats set off up the Nile from here.

SETTING THE SCENE

Egypt in the height of blistering summer heat might be less than welcoming. The Egyptians, however, are a friendly, hospitable people, who welcome foreign nationals with open arms. There's just one vital thing to be aware of – they're fanatical about personal hygiene and cleanliness. In the hot, dusty climate, with sand which gets everywhere, Egyptians spend hours washing themselves and their clothes. Keep as clean as they do and you'll fit right in.

QUIRKY QUOTES

Some pages have quotes, giving the views of visitors and Ancient Egyptians, shown like the one here:

66 Would that I were in the country always... **99**

Taken from an early manuscript

TIPS FOR TOURISTS

Finally, on most pages you'll find helpful hints in a box like this:

TOP TIPS FOR TOURISTS

No. 1: Red letter days

The Egyptian calendar is full of "good" and "bad" days marked in red (which were days when good or bad things had happened to their gods). Don't do anything at all on a bad day. It may end in disaster.

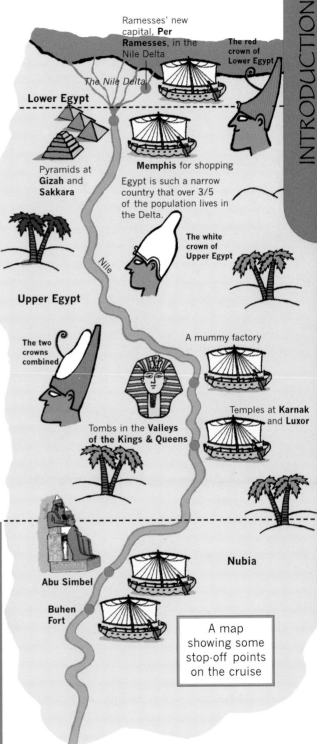

Ramesses' new capital, **Per Ramesses**, in the Nile Delta

The red crown of Lower Egypt

The Nile Delta

Lower Egypt

Pyramids at **Gizah** and **Sakkara**

Memphis for shopping

Egypt is such a narrow country that over 3/5 of the population lives in the Delta.

The white crown of **Upper Egypt**

Nile

Upper Egypt

The two crowns combined

A mummy factory

Temples at **Karnak** and **Luxor**

Tombs in the **Valleys of the Kings & Queens**

Abu Simbel

Buhen Fort

Nubia

A map showing some stop-off points on the cruise

PRACTICALITIES

Tourism in Ancient Egypt won't take off until the Greeks arrive in the 6th century BC. Though you'll see the country in its unspoiled glory, you'll be fending for yourself. There are no hotels, no tour guides and no embassy if you hit trouble.

If you still want to visit, the best times to go are October or March, either side of the extreme summer heat. In March, you have the added bonus of harvest festivals.

A fan is vital, though this one is so heavy, it needs a servant to carry it.

WHAT TO WEAR

For clothes, think little and loose. Egypt is very hot, though it's a dry, not humid, heat. Most people wear white linen tunics or robes, though working men just wear a loincloth. Make your first stop a market to buy a tunic. You won't need wet weather gear as it hardly ever rains.

TOP TIPS FOR TOURISTS

No. 2: Ouch!

Check your shoes for scorpions before putting them on. There are few snakes in Egypt, though be warned: those that do live there are extremely dangerous, so keep your distance.

PACKING

Since you'll be moving around, travel light. There are just three essentials to keep with you at all times: a fan, insect repellent and, believe it or not, pepper: see "Bartering (& Bribes)".

If you don't bring insect repellent, a palm leaf will have to do.

BARTERING (& BRIBES)

A basic money system using copper weights is in place, but generally goods and services are simply bartered (exchanged). Even wages are paid in food. Take a plentiful supply of spices – they're a popular currency. You'll get a good rate of exchange for pepper and silk, as the Egyptians don't have either. Not only will you need goods to buy things, they're also useful as presents. Many places aren't officially open, but guards will show you around in return for a suitable "gift".

EMERGENCIES

If you have an emergency, call the equivalent of the police: the *Medjay*. There are Medjay in all the major towns, keeping law and order, catching criminals and guarding the frontiers.

The Medjay use "sniffer" dogs to track down criminals.

MEASURES

The main unit of measurement is a *cubit*, which is the distance from an adult's elbow to his or her fingertips. Measurements vary, depending on whose arm is used, so there's also a *Royal Cubit* (52.5cm or 21in), which is standard across the country.

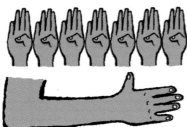

For smaller measurements, spans (hands) or digits (fingers) are used. Seven spans or 28 digits make a cubit.

WEIGHTS

Egyptian weights are stones or pieces of metal, often shaped like animals. The basic weight is a *deben* which weighs about 91g (3.64oz). One deben is made up of ten *kites*; ten debens (100 kites) make a *sep*.

TIME

Time is measured using water clocks. Water drains out of a pot divided into hour-long sections. The Egyptians have a 24 hour day.

THE CALENDAR

Twelve months of thirty days each, plus five holy days stuck on the end, make the 365 day year. There are ten days in a week, with every tenth day a holiday. Years are numbered from the start of a king's reign. When Ramesses II took the throne, the calendar went back to Year 1.

THE SEASONS

There are three seasons, based on the farming year. **Inundation** (July - October) is the annual flooding of the Nile, without which all of Egypt would be a barren desert. **Planting** lasts from November to February, and **Harvest** from March to June.

The floods fertilize land either side of the Nile.

GETTING AROUND

gypt's major highway isn't a road at all but a river, the Nile. With roads virtually non-existent, and wheeled vehicles few and far between, it's your best bet for getting from one place to another.

Most villages are near the Nile, and temples on the desert edge are connected to it by a network of canals. You'll find journeying by river is efficient and very reliable. (Which may be a change from getting around back home.)

BOATING

Because boats are the main way to travel, there's a wide choice, from ferries to cargo ships and grain barges. Ferrymen ply their trade between east and west banks, charging a couple of small copper weights at most.

CRUISING

For a longer trip up the Nile, jump on a boat heading south. The most luxurious are the royal barges. You're unlikely to hitch a ride on one of these, but you may be able to talk your way on to an official's state ship. Otherwise, don't expect the equivalent of a modern cruise ship. You'll be lucky if your boat has a canopy. You'll wash in the river and eat and sleep on the river bank – but you wouldn't want to be stuck in a stifling cabin. Besides, sitting on an open deck is the best way to see the countryside.

To tell if a boat is going south, look for a sail. The current flows downstream (north), while the prevailing wind blows upstream (south). So, boats heading south need sails, while those going north use oars.

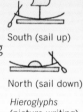

South (sail up)

North (sail down)

Hieroglyphs (picture writing)

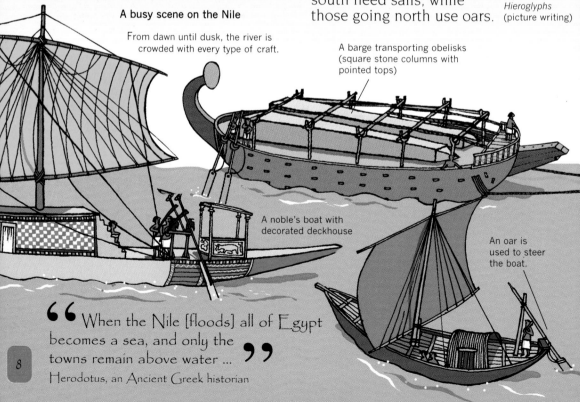

A busy scene on the Nile

From dawn until dusk, the river is crowded with every type of craft.

A barge transporting obelisks (square stone columns with pointed tops)

A noble's boat with decorated deckhouse

An oar is used to steer the boat.

66 When the Nile [floods] all of Egypt becomes a sea, and only the towns remain above water ... 99
Herodotus, an Ancient Greek historian

LAND TRAVEL

Few roads exist, and those that do are all within towns. There's no point having roads link one town to another. They'd simply be washed away every year with the floods. Not only that, farmers need what little land there is for raising crops.

If you pictured yourself sweeping across the desert on a camel, think again. Camels won't arrive in Egypt until about 600BC – and won't be used for travel for 300 years after that. Horses are an option, but too expensive for most people. In town, you might be able to rent a chariot – or even a carrying chair – but the distances are so small it's hardly worth it.

Carrying chairs are totally impractical on desert sand.

TOP TIPS FOR TOURISTS

No. 3: Desert storm

NEVER agree to a tour of the desert with a friendly "guide". You'll be robbed before you've gone a few steps. Coming back (if you're left alive), you'll almost certainly get lost. One Persian general lost his entire army in the desert. It was never seen again.

If you venture further afield on land, take a string of donkeys carrying plenty of drinking water. Dehydration (lack of water) is a constant problem. Two pharaohs had wells built on the way to some gold mines in the eastern desert, but it's a long way between oases (pools of water) in the western desert.

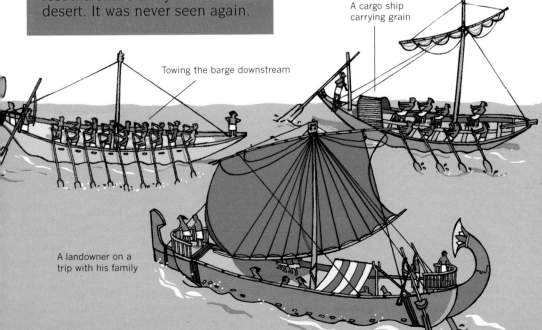

A cargo ship carrying grain

Towing the barge downstream

A landowner on a trip with his family

WHERE TO STAY

For most of the vacation, you'll be sleeping on (or beside) a boat. But for your forays onto dry land, there are no hotels and the inns are best avoided: many are simply beer houses with (very) rowdy customers. Your only course of action is to rent somewhere.

TOWN PLANNING

Renting a townhouse or apartment isn't the most restful option. Towns are crowded, busy, noisy and dirty, with buildings crammed together. Most towns sprang up piecemeal. Even the few that are planned don't last, as each generation builds on top of the ones before.

A scene from a typical town

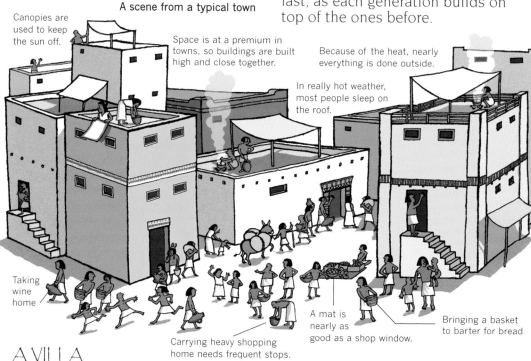

Canopies are used to keep the sun off.

Space is at a premium in towns, so buildings are built high and close together.

Because of the heat, nearly everything is done outside.

In really hot weather, most people sleep on the roof.

Taking wine home

A mat is nearly as good as a shop window.

Bringing a basket to barter for bread

Carrying heavy shopping home needs frequent stops.

A VILLA

Most people live in three or four-roomed houses, though townhouses, with several floors, are generally bigger. If you can afford it, go for the villa of an official working away from home. This will come with household staff, including cooks, and, if you're lucky, a chariot and horses in the stable.

The garden, with sunshade, is at the front of the villa. Storage space and the cooking area are at the back.

Most villas follow the layout shown here.

Bedrooms

Animal pens

The central room is largest and is used for entertaining.

All houses, including villas, are built from bricks of mud and straw.

FURNITURE

There's a limited range of furniture, but it's of a surprisingly modern design and a good standard of craftsmanship. Like everything else in Egypt, the more costly an item, the better it is made and the more expensive the materials used.

Basics include stools, tables, and chairs – though these are only for the most important people in the house. Beds are a wooden frame, with linen sheets. The "pillows" may come as a shock. They're just wooden (or even stone) headrests.

The Egyptians find the headrests very comfortable, but you may prefer to use a cushion.

Oil-burning lamps are decorative – but not very bright.

AIR CONDITIONING

In a country where the heat is intense, only the very rich have air conditioning. In Egypt, this means a servant with a fan. The few concessions to the heat are air vents in the roof, to catch what breeze there is, and tiny windows set high up in the walls, which let in as little sun as possible. Walls are thick and often whitewashed on the outside to reflect the heat.

PUBLIC AMENITIES

There's no state sewage or refuse collection. You'll be throwing your waste into pits (or occasionally the river or street) like everyone else. It's the one time you'll be grateful for the heat. Refuse dries up so quickly that smells don't have a chance to linger. There's no running water either. All water is collected from private or public wells and carried to the house. If you're exceptionally lucky, your villa will have its own well.

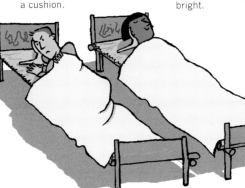

"BATH" ROOM

Better properties have bathrooms, though there are no bathtubs, just a toilet and "shower". Walls are lined with limestone to protect them from splashes, as the shower is a servant pouring a jug of water over you. The toilet, though, is a wooden seat over a large clay pot filled with sand. The pot is taken away to be emptied.

TOP TIPS FOR TOURISTS

No. 4: Feeling lost?

Try not to be confused by the lack of street names and numbers. Egyptians find their way around with reference to other buildings near the place they want to go. Get into the habit of memorizing the location of useful landmarks.

FOOD & DRINK

If you take a vacation for a rest from cooking, you're in for a let-down. In Egypt, you'll be self-catering. There are no cafés, only a few snack stands offering bread, meat and beer. If you can't cook, or don't want to slave over a hot fire without a dozen electrical gadgets on hand, rent a villa with servants to do it for you.

BREAD AND BEER

Bread and beer, made from wheat and/or barley, are the staples of everyone's diet, no matter what their age or class. It's made Egyptian bakers inventive – you'll find more than 40 types of bread and cakes on offer. Bread often comes with added extras, such as honey, garlic or herbs.

Even peasants have a better diet than other ancient peoples, because Egypt's agriculture is so rich. For the wealthier Egyptian or tourist, the choice is wider still. The cooking oil, made from linseed, saffron, sesame (and sometimes olives), adds a distinctive taste to dishes. So does honey – used to sweeten things as there's no sugar.

This mountain of food from a tomb painting shows onions, pomegranates, cucumbers, grapes, ducks and fish – the diet of a wealthy Egyptian.

MEAT EATERS

Meat includes mutton, goat, and pork (unless you're a priest). Beef is available, but expensive and only for special occasions. As there's little grazing land, the cows are small, so mainly kept for milk, which is used for cheese. There's a huge variety of fish and fowl, fresh and dried. But don't look for chickens. They're such rare birds, the pharaoh exhibits them in his private zoo.

VEGETARIANS

Fruit and vegetables grow in abundance and include beans, lentils, radishes, garlic, peas, grapes, figs, pomegranates and dates – so you certainly won't lack variety if you don't eat meat. There are also plenty of eggs, nuts and cheese for protein.

TOP TIPS FOR TOURISTS

No. 5: Toothpick

Be careful when you're eating bread. It's made outside and the dough picks up no end of grit and stones – which are then baked in along with the seeds. Not only does this wear down your teeth, you may end up losing a few.

DRINKS

Beer is made from crumbled bread and water, and so lumpy it's strained before serving. More expensive is the wine, made from dates, grapes or pomegranates. Wine labels give the vineyard, year of produce and a comment, such as "very very good".

Apart from beer and wine, there's water. This is safe to drink, either from wells or, amazingly, straight from the Nile. There are no ice cubes, so, to cool the water down, simply let it drip from one clay pot into another.

A drinking straw

Beer is drunk through large wooden straws with filters. Even after straining, it remains full of lumps.

COOKING

Because of the heat and fire risk, all cooking takes place outside. If you take turns cooking, bear in mind that only women bake bread.

FAN THE FLAMES

Large joints of meat are turned on a spit, often over a brazier (metal container) filled with charcoal. The most common fuels though are sticks, dried grass and reeds. Reeds give short, sharp bursts of heat, but need constant fanning to keep alight.

> **66** I have been over this blaze since the world began. I never saw such a [huge] duck! **99**
>
> XII Dynasty cook

Cooking al fresco

Most Egyptians cook on a tripod (three-legged stand) over a fire.

Loaves are formed into rounds and stuck on the outside of the oven. They fall off when cooked.

To keep a fire going, someone has to fan the flames. (It helps if someone fans him.)

GETTING SICK

ncient Egypt isn't a bad place to be if you're ill. The Egyptians' belief in hygiene and their logical approach to medicine reach a standard not seen again until the 1800s (AD). That said, it's better to have an obvious problem, such as a gashed arm, than appendicitis.

Egyptian doctors have a widespread reputation for excellence, some working as far afield as Babylon. Most work as general practitioners, though there are also specialists who focus on specific parts of the body.

VISITING A DOCTOR

Much like home, doctors observe symptoms, ask questions and examine their patients before making a diagnosis. Everything is recorded on papyrus (the Egyptian form of paper), so there's a record for the future. These notes are stored in vast medical libraries in temples, which doctors are free to consult. If your doctor hasn't a clue, he'll be upfront about that too.

SURGERY

If you need an operation, your chances of survival are fairly high. Instruments are always sterilized in flames and surgeons keep both their patients and surroundings clean. Fractures are healed with splints and casts, and open wounds are closed with stitches and clamps. There's even an anesthetic made from poppies, which doubles as a painkiller.

A knife used in surgery and a pair of iron tweezers

A TEXTBOOK CASE

What in later years will become known as the "Edwin Smith" papyrus has 48 case studies, and may date back to the Third Dynasty. Doctors use it to check a range of complaints from wounds to fractures.

❝ This is an ailment I can treat. This is an ailment I will try to treat. This is an ailment not to be treated. **❞**

You'll hear one of these three statements before diagnosis.

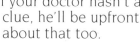

One king brought his entire family over from Canaan, just to consult an Egyptian doctor.

MEDICAL MANUALS

There are papyruses on surgery, anatomy and pharmacy (the use of drugs). All drugs are natural (animal, plant or mineral-based) and some are surprisingly effective. In fact, Nile mud, a popular ingredient, has an antibiotic in it.

MEDICINE & RELIGION

All treatment, even for a broken limb, involves prayer. The Egyptians are highly religious and believe that everything they do should have the blessing of the gods. If all else fails, go to a temple and ask to sleep there. You may not undergo a miraculous recovery, but with luck you'll dream the cure.

Even if you dream a cure, you may still need a priest to interpret its meaning.

INTERNAL ORGANS

Much of the knowledge doctors have of internal organs comes from mummification (the technique used to preserve a body after death). Doctors know that the heart pumps blood and say of the pulse, "It speaks the messages of the heart." But they vastly overrate the heart's importance. They believe it the source of intelligence, ignoring the brain. They even think that the stomach is connected to the heart.

> **66** O... Isis... come and see your father concerning that enemy, dead man or dead woman, which is in the head of N... **99**

A charm for curing a headache caused by a spirit inside the head

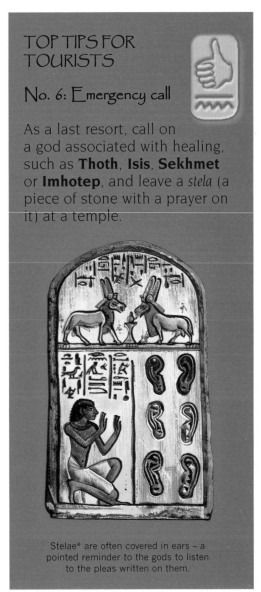

TOP TIPS FOR TOURISTS

No. 6: Emergency call

As a last resort, call on a god associated with healing, such as **Thoth**, **Isis**, **Sekhmet** or **Imhotep**, and leave a *stela* (a piece of stone with a prayer on it) at a temple.

Stelae* are often covered in ears – a pointed reminder to the gods to listen to the pleas written on them.

*Stelae is the plural of stela

THE GREAT PYRAMIDS

First stop on the river cruise is one of the most spectacular sights you'll see, on this trip or any other – the Great Pyramids, already over 1,000 years old. Located at **Gizah**, they're a popular day-out for the Ancient Egyptians too.

They were built for three pharaohs of the Fourth Dynasty (Khufu, Khafre and Menkaure; also known as Cheops, Chephren and Mycerinus) as giant tombs for their mummified bodies.

Building a pyramid

Blocks are pulled on oiled rollers.

PYRAMID FACTS

The largest pyramid was built for Khufu c.2500BC. At 140m (460ft) tall, it's taller than 24 giraffes on top of each other, and contains more than 2.5 million blocks. These were cut so precisely, the gaps between them are less than 0.5mm (1/32 inch) wide. The pyramid is encased in limestone which gleams a dazzling white in the sun.

The Grand Gallery: a shaft leading to Khufu's chamber (see diagram on right)

THE WORKFORCE

A pyramid took about 20 years to build, but it wasn't built by suffering slaves. The builders were free men and, though it was hard work, each man only worked on the project for a short time. Besides, he was fed, clothed and housed by the king; the work reduced his tax bill; and it pleased the gods.

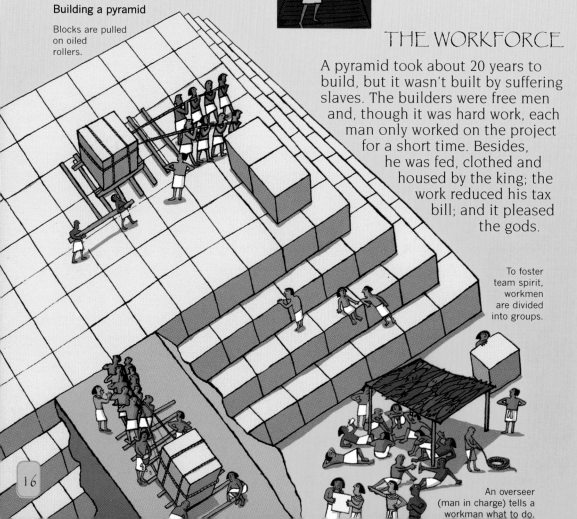

To foster team spirit, workmen are divided into groups.

An overseer (man in charge) tells a workman what to do.

TOMB ROBBERS

Egyptians believe in a life after death, so pharaohs are buried with everything they might need in that next life, plus numerous valuables. It means the pyramids are – or were – a treasure trove. Huge stone blocks were used to seal off their entrances but, spurred on by the thought of all that gold, thieves got in anyway. Even now, halfway through the New Kingdom, most pyramids have been cleaned out.

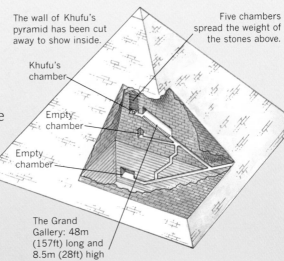

The wall of Khufu's pyramid has been cut away to show inside.

Five chambers spread the weight of the stones above.

Khufu's chamber

Empty chamber

Empty chamber

The Grand Gallery: 48m (157ft) long and 8.5m (28ft) high

PYRAMID TEMPLES

Upon arrival at the pyramids, you may well moor near to the Valley Temple on the bank of the Nile. This is where the pharaoh's body was brought on its final journey from the palace. The body was carried down the Nile in a *barque* (funeral boat), which was then buried beside the pyramid.

A covered road links the Valley Temple with a second temple, the Mortuary Temple, built in front of the pyramid. For hundreds of years, this temple was visited daily by priests with food for the dead pharaoh to sustain him in the afterlife.

The Sphinx, whose face is said to have been based on King Khafre's

TOP TIPS FOR TOURISTS
No. 7: Souvenirs

Don't buy anything from one of the many sellers hawking "genuine" souvenirs outside the pyramids. One: it's illegal. Two: whether they're pyramid stone or "royal jewels", they're undoubtedly fakes.

GUARDIAN OF GIZAH

Standing guard over the pyramids, though not that effectively, is the enigmatic Sphinx. At the start of the New Kingdom, it was buried under sand. You'll see it on your trip thanks to a young prince (later Tuthmosis IV), who dreamed if he cleared it, he would be king.

STEP PYRAMIDS

Think of a pyramid and you'll probably picture the straight-sided ones at Gizah, pointing to the sky. But your next stop off, **Sakkara**, is home to some different pyramids, the first ever built.

Sakkara, south of Gizah, is the necropolis (cemetery) for Memphis, the capital of the Old Kingdom. The largest of the cemeteries, it contains 15 royal pyramids. King of them all is the one built for Djoser, a pharaoh at the start of the Third Dynasty.

SIX STEPS TO HEAVEN

Originally, pharaohs were buried in mud-brick buildings called *mastabas*. Then, Djoser's architect, Imhotep, designed a tomb made of stone that would revolutionize burials.

Taking a stone mastaba as his starting point, he enlarged it and built five more on top, each one smaller than the one beneath. This formed a "step" pyramid of six layers, popularly said to represent the pharaoh's stepladder to heaven.

A step pyramid

The buildings around the edge are finely carved on the outside, but the insides are full of rubble.

The pyramid is set in a vast complex, 547m (1,790ft) by 278m (912ft). Most of the other buildings are for decoration only.

The "Heb Sed" court, where the king celebrates the festival of "Sed" (see page 51).

TOP TIPS FOR TOURISTS

No. 8: Steps to prison

Tempting though the steps may be, don't try to climb them (as tourists from later centuries will). It's the height of disrespect and you could end up somewhere that's the very opposite of heaven.

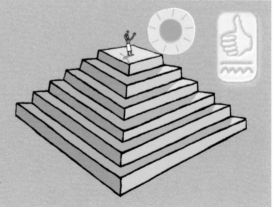

PYRAMID TEXTS

Look out especially for Unas' pyramid. (Unas was a pharaoh of the Fifth Dynasty.) If you can get inside, do. The interior walls were the first to be covered in hieroglyphic messages, containing chants and spells. These were meant to protect and help the pharaoh on his hazardous journey through *Duat* (the underworld) to the afterlife.

Stonemasons painstakingly carve text onto the interior walls of a tomb.

FROM STONE TO PAPER

These wall spells, known as *Pyramid Texts*, were strictly for pharaohs only. Years later, the idea was adopted by private individuals, who painted charms onto their coffins. These were termed *Coffin Texts*. Since the beginning of the New Kingdom, they have been inscribed on sheets of papyrus and are called the *Book of the Dead* (see page 33).

"LIVING" CEMETERY

Sakkara is more than a site for ancient pyramids though. You may see a burial taking place during your visit. (In fact, it will go on being used as a cemetery right up to the 21st century.)

All the tombs are decorated with wall paintings and painted reliefs (wall carvings).

A NOBLE GRAVEYARD

Some of the mastabas just north of Djoser's pyramid go back even earlier, to the First Dynasty. But these belong to various nobles and court officials. First and Second Dynasty pharaohs were buried in a royal cemetery at Abydos, close to the town of Thebes in Upper Egypt.

Kings only began to be buried at Sakkara from the start of the Third Dynasty, when the royal burial ground was moved here. These pharaohs' tombs are surrounded by hundreds of others, belonging to members of the royal household and their families.

Currently, pharaohs are buried in the **Valley of the Kings** on the West Bank (see pages 24-25) but some officials are still entombed here. If, during your visit, a tomb is being prepared for one of Ramesses' courtiers, you may even get the chance to look around inside.

Tomb walls show scenes from everyday life, such as boat builders hard at work.

THE SIGHTS OF MEMPHIS

Halfway between the burial sites of Sakkara and Gizah lies **Memphis**, Egypt's capital during the Old Kingdom. Still the country's key administrative headquarters, Memphis is at the heart of Egypt's thriving import/export industry. It's grown since Menes founded it – see how small it was by following the dazzling white walls which enclosed the early city. You can easily spend several days here, if you can stand the noise. There's masses to see and buy, cheap imports in particular.

Manufactured goods from Greece

Copper from Cyprus

Timber, olive oil and resin from the Lebanon

Silver, horses and slaves from Syria

Memphis

Salt from oases

Ebony and ivory from Africa

Wine from Libya

Lapis lazuli from Afghanistan

EGYPT

Incense from Punt (in East Africa)

Gold from Nubia

A map of Egypt's imports

A scene in a Memphis market

Sheets of copper shaped like animal hides

Traders exchanging news

Traders come from all over the Mediterranean to sell their goods.

Goods are spread out on mats on the ground.

Terracotta urns and enamel flasks

FOREIGN TRADE

Just below the Nile Delta, Memphis is in the perfect spot for trade. Many traders settle here, giving the city a cosmopolitan feel. Mingling with the merchants you'll find everyone from foreign dignitaries bearing gold tributes for the king, to peasants from oases with blocks of salt, and rushes for baskets.

Visit the docks to see boats being loaded with papyrus and linen for export by *shwty* (government traders). Imports include cedar from the Lebanon – vital in view of Egypt's lack of tall trees. There are even shrines for foreign gods, an example of the Egyptians' liberal "Pray and let pray" attitude to religion.

THE TEMPLE OF PTAH

As you'd expect of so great a city, Memphis has its own god – and not just any god. According to Memphisians, their god Ptah (say "tar") created the world by saying the name of each thing in turn, bringing it to life. Whether you believe this or not, his temple is one of the largest in Egypt.

The god Ptah creating life

South of the temple is an enclosure where you can see the famous **Apis bull** – believed to be Ptah in an earthly form. (Gods are so powerful, they can't be seen in their true form, so an animal is chosen for the god's spirit to reside in.) Each time the bull dies, all of Egypt is scoured for a replacement. The lucky bull that fits the correct description gets to live like a god.

The Apis bull is always black and white, with a white pyramid on his forehead and a vulture-shaped patch on his back.

HELIOPOLIS

Only a short boat ride away, and definitely worth the trip, is the town of **Heliopolis**. It houses the temple of Re the Sun God. This temple is open to let in the sun, so you'll get a good view. Look for the obelisk in the third courtyard, with a copy of the "Benben" stone at the top. Said to be a gift from Re, the stone fell flaming from the sky (so it's probably a meteorite). You may even see Re himself. Like Ptah, his earthly form is a bull, known as the **Mnevis bull**.

The obelisk topped with a copy of the Benben stone

TOP TIPS FOR TOURISTS

No. 9: Agony uncle

Something worrying you? Visit the **Apis bull**. You can ask him any question you like, as long as the answer is *yes* or *no*. Go to the courtyard where the bull is to be paraded (follow the crowd) and give a priest your question. In front of the bull stand identical feeding troughs, marked *Yes* and *No*. When the priest asks your question, the trough the bull eats from gives your answer.

TEMPLES

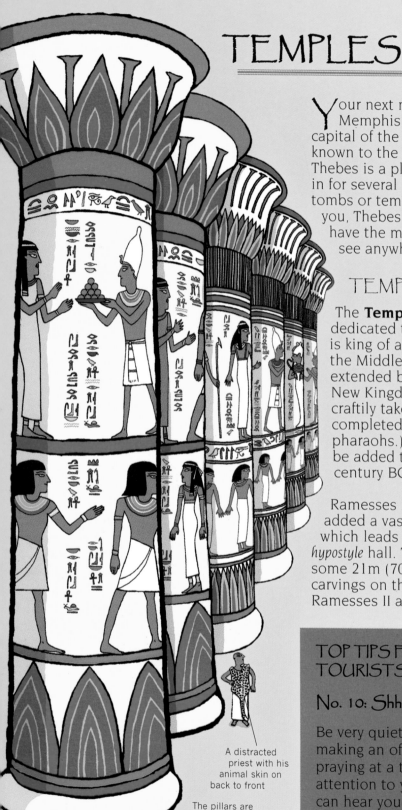

Your next major stop after Memphis is **Thebes**, religious capital of the New Kingdom (and known to the Egyptians as *Waset*). Thebes is a place you'll want to stay in for several days. Whether it's tombs or temples which interest you, Thebes and nearby **Karnak** have the most magnificent you'll see anywhere.

TEMPLE OF AMUN

The **Temple of Amun** at Karnak, dedicated to the king of the gods, is king of all temples. Begun in the Middle Kingdom, it has been extended by each dynasty of the New Kingdom. (Ramesses II has craftily taken the credit for work completed by previous pharaohs.) It will continue to be added to, well into the first century BC.

Ramesses II himself has added a vast *pylon*, or gateway, which leads to the renowned *hypostyle* hall. This has 134 columns, some 21m (70ft) tall. Look for the carvings on the outer walls, showing Ramesses II and his father in battle.

A distracted priest with his animal skin on back to front

The pillars are carved with scenes of pharaohs making offerings to the gods.

TOP TIPS FOR TOURISTS

No. 10: Shhh!

Be very quiet when making an offering or praying at a temple. Don't draw attention to yourself. The gods can hear you perfectly well – and no one else wants to.

LUXOR TEMPLE

South of Karnak is **Luxor**, a smaller, simpler temple, though no less impressive. It's here that the annual festival of **Opet** takes place (see page 51). Amenhotep III built the temple in 1380 BC. Ramesses is currently adding a pylon gate, a courtyard and his trademark: huge statues. At the entrance stand two huge obelisks, though by the 19th century only one will remain. The other will be sent to Paris in 1831.

The Temple of Luxor

An avenue of sphinxes leads from Karnak to Luxor.

A TEMPLE LAYOUT

Every town or village has at least one temple, dedicated to a particular god. Some temples are vast complexes, others are more basic, but they all have the same layout. At the entrance is an open courtyard – which is as far as most people get. For those allowed in, a *hypostyle* hall leads to the shrine.

KEEP OUT!

Theoretically, the only person who can make offerings to the gods is the pharaoh, a god himself. In practice, he delegates to priests. So, as a rule, only the pharaoh and his priests – the servants of a god – may enter a temple.

Inside a temple

Obelisk

Hypostyle hall

Shrine with a statue of the temple's god

Courtyard

Schoolroom, workshops and store rooms

Sacred pool where priests get water to purify themselves

VALLEY OF THE KINGS

The pyramids proved too spectacular for their own good: they were all robbed. So, for over 200 years, kings have been buried in secret tombs in the **Valley of the Kings**. These are in cliffs at West Thebes, on the edge of the western desert. The area is dominated by "The Peak", a pyramid-shaped mountain on which the deadly cobra goddess *Merit-Seger* is said to live. She resents intruders – but tomb robbers don't give up easily.

BUILDING A TOMB

The tomb site for each pharaoh is chosen soon after he takes the throne, and work begins immediately. Plans are drawn up and orders are sent to the workers. If you go to watch them, take plenty of water. Loose rock and sand are dug out with chisels and wooden mallets and it's a dusty business. The work is hot and tiring and space is limited, so don't get in the way.

Tomb builders hard at work

Tombs are lit by linen wicks burning in saucers of animal fat.

TOP TIPS FOR TOURISTS

No. 11: Stop thief!

Don't wander around alone. Guards are on constant patrol. Anyone not at work is treated with suspicion. To be on the safe side, offer the Medjay a gift and ask for a tour.

As well as the diggers, there are workers checking that the walls, roof and floors are straight, porters dragging baskets of stone away, and painters and plasterers hard at work. Occasionally, sheets of polished metal are used to reflect sunlight into the tombs, making the tombs brighter. It's an impressive trick if you can find someone with the time to show you.

"THE VILLAGE"

If you spend a few days exploring the area, you'll probably stay in **The Village** (Deir El-Medina in modern times). It's the purpose-built estate for the tomb workers, with the Valley of the Kings on one side and the **Valley of the Queens** on the other.

The path between the tombs and estate is a difficult trek, so workers sleep in huts by the tombs for the working week, returning home to their families for the weekend. You could rent a worker's house, though they tend to be airless with little light. (Windows are simply tiny slits by the ceiling.)

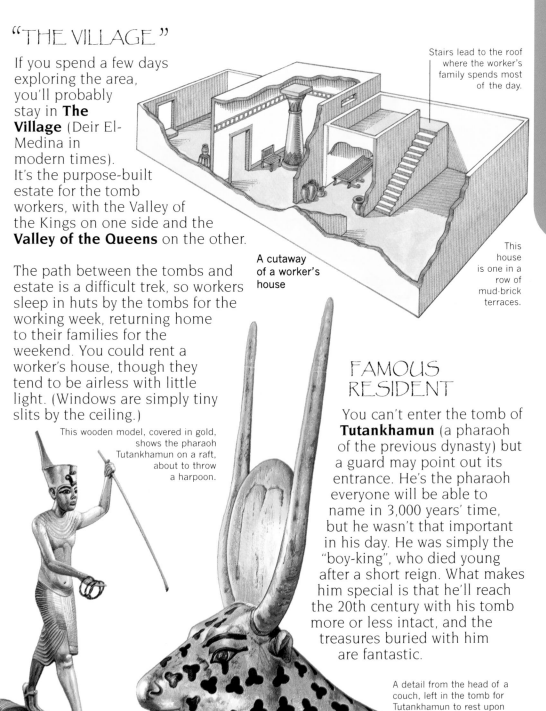

Stairs lead to the roof where the worker's family spends most of the day.

A cutaway of a worker's house

This house is one in a row of mud-brick terraces.

This wooden model, covered in gold, shows the pharaoh Tutankhamun on a raft, about to throw a harpoon.

FAMOUS RESIDENT

You can't enter the tomb of **Tutankhamun** (a pharaoh of the previous dynasty) but a guard may point out its entrance. He's the pharaoh everyone will be able to name in 3,000 years' time, but he wasn't that important in his day. He was simply the "boy-king", who died young after a short reign. What makes him special is that he'll reach the 20th century with his tomb more or less intact, and the treasures buried with him are fantastic.

A detail from the head of a couch, left in the tomb for Tutankhamun to rest upon

TOMB ART

Called "Place of Beauty" by the Egyptians, the **Valley of the Queens** is the burial site for the pharaohs' wives and offspring. The major tomb currently being built here is for Nefertari, chief wife of Ramesses II. Try to visit it if you can – but you'll need to be persuasive with the workmen. Some of the finest examples of Egyptian art are found in tombs. Nefertari's will be one of the best.

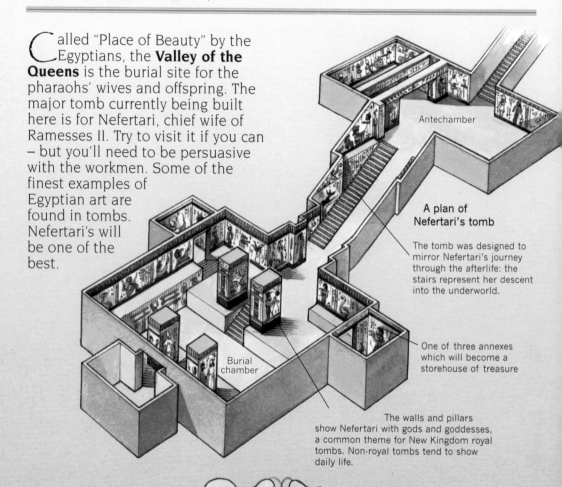

Antechamber

A plan of Nefertari's tomb

The tomb was designed to mirror Nefertari's journey through the afterlife: the stairs represent her descent into the underworld.

One of three annexes which will become a storehouse of treasure

Burial chamber

The walls and pillars show Nefertari with gods and goddesses, a common theme for New Kingdom royal tombs. Non-royal tombs tend to show daily life.

ANCIENT ART

To the Egyptians, art isn't mere representation. Images of people or objects don't just show them, they can replace them. In other words, a picture of fruit on your tomb wall is as good as having the fruit itself. Because of this, an artist aims to tell you as much about the subject as possible. This means Egyptian paintings don't always look that realistic.

A painting of a box with things inside, shows the things on top, so you can see what they are. No object overlaps another, so no detail is hidden from view. Different viewpoints are also combined, the most obvious example being people, who are drawn with their faces in profile but their shoulders full on.

A bearer with offerings from a wall painting on a tomb at Thebes

PAINTING A TOMB

To paint a tomb, plasterers first smooth the walls with clay and apply a layer of plaster. A carefully measured grid is painted on top, using string dipped in red paint. Teams of artists do the first sketch in red, following a plan drawn on squared papyrus. A master artist then corrects mistakes in black ink.

Wall carvings are common in royal tombs. You'll probably see a sculptor carving around the outlines to make them stand out. At this stage, the wall is covered in another, finer layer of plaster before the scenes are painted. Finally, the outlines are gone over once more and details are added with a fine brush.

The different stages of tomb painting

Oil in the lamps is mixed with salt so that the wicks don't smoke and spoil the painting.

Painting the first sketch

This sculptor is making a *raised* carving, cutting away the background so that the figure stands out.

Checking the plan

Mixing paint

MIXING PAINT

Paints are made from minerals such as clay and iron oxide (ochre which gives reds and yellows); malachite (greens); silica, copper and calcium (blue); soot (black) and limestone (white). The dry minerals are pounded to a powder with a pestle and mortar and mixed with gum or egg white to make them liquid.

PERFECT PEOPLE

People are generally shown in an idealized fashion, because this is how they want to look in the afterlife. Study the paintings of Egyptian figures and you'll notice they all look alike. Men and women are always 18 squares tall from their hairlines to the soles of their feet, with their features at set points.

GODS & GODDESSES

The gods are considered so glorious and all-powerful, they cannot be seen with the human eye. To get around this, they appear on earth disguised in animal form. The Egyptians have enormous faith in their gods and goddesses, seeking advice, help or approval on a daily basis. They pray to hundreds, both local (who are unheard of outside a particular region) and national.

You can use this page as a quick reference for the main gods you'll come across when visiting tombs.

AMUN-RE

Two gods for the price of one, **Amun-Re** was originally **Re**, Sun God and King of Egypt, and **Amun**, god of Thebes. When Thebes was made the capital of Egypt, the two merged to become chief god and protector of the pharaoh.

TOP TIPS FOR TOURISTS

No. 12: Don't say his name!

Only once, under **Akhenaten**, did Egypt almost become a one-god nation. Akhenaten promoted a sun god, Aten, above all others, but the scheme lasted as long as his reign. His reputation is now so low that the penalty for anyone even saying his name is severe.

Amun-Re

OSIRIS

Osiris is the King of the Underworld and the second most important god. He was the first to die and live again, the ambition of every Egyptian. His temple is at Abydos where he is said to have been buried.

THE STORY OF OSIRIS

Osiris was one of the earliest kings of Egypt. Much beloved, he taught his people how to grow crops. But he was tricked and murdered by his jealous brother Set. Osiris's sister-wife Isis found his body but, when she returned with it, Set simply cut it up. Refusing to give in, Isis collected every part. With the help of Anubis, she mummified Osiris and brought him back to life.

Osiris

Today, all mummies are prepared in the same way, in the hope that they, too, will come back to life. Osiris's face was even painted green to symbolize regrowth and rebirth. Figures of Osiris, made from mud and sown with wheat seed, are often left in tombs. It's thought that the new life, growing in the form of wheat, will be extra encouragement.

BEST OF THE REST

Isis: devoted sister-wife of Osiris and protector of women, Egyptian women look up to her as a model wife and mother. In recent times, her importance has grown.

Set: Osiris's evil brother, he's god of trouble, the desert and storms. Animals associated with him are pigs, donkeys and male hippos.

Horus: son of Osiris and Isis, he inherited the throne after his father's death. (Now, all kings become the living embodiment of Horus on ascending the throne.) Sometimes shown with a falcon's head, his main temple is at Edfu.

Hathor: Horus's wife. Currently eclipsed by Isis, she's an important, ancient goddess of music, beauty and love. Her sacred animal is a cow.

Bes: a dwarf and the jester of the gods, he also looks the most approachable. He protects the house and family, especially children. Though he has no temple of his own, there are models of him in most homes.

Tawaret: a pregnant hippo, who, as you'd expect, is the goddess of pregnancy and childbirth.

Ma'at: goddess of

truth and justice, harmony and the balance of the Universe. She's usually shown in human form but sometimes represented by a feather.

Anubis: jackal-headed god of the dead and mummification, and guardian of cemeteries. (Jackals look like dogs.)

Thoth: god of the moon, wisdom and healing, and patron of scribes (officials who can write). Mathematicians, engineers and officials all worship Thoth. According to legend, he wrote 42 volumes containing all the wisdom in the world.

Ptah: the god of craftsmen, whose main temple is at Memphis. He's married to **Sekhmet**.

Sekhmet: the goddess who avenges wrongs done to Re. A destructive and feared deity, she also cures disease with her breath.

A MUMMY FACTORY

Conjure up an image of Ancient Egypt and you'll probably picture mummies, the embalmed (preserved) bodies of dead Egyptians. Though, strictly speaking, a tour around a "mummy factory" isn't available to visitors, doors will open in return for a "gift".

WHY A "MUMMY"?

All Egyptians believe life continues after death. But, to enjoy the afterlife fully, their bodies must survive. This need for a body after death led to mummification, a drying out of the body to preserve it. Don't call them mummies, though. The name will only catch on when they're discovered in the 19th century AD. The mummies' blackened skin (from embalming resin) made their Arab discoverers believe they'd been coated in *mummiya*, a kind of tar.

LAND OF THE DEAD

Soon after death, bodies are taken to the west bank of the Nile. This desert area where the sun sets is thought of as the land of the dead. Here, they are washed and purified before being taken to a building, the *wabet*, to be embalmed. If you get into a wabet, be respectful. You are watching a sacred rite, after all.

Unless you have a couple of months, you'll have to see the various stages of embalming on different bodies. Proper embalming takes up to 70 days, though services range from deluxe to very cheap. The poor are preserved in less than a week.

TOP TIPS FOR TOURISTS

No.13: An iron stomach

Even grown men pale at the sight of someone's brains being pulled through their nostrils. Plan your visit carefully, that is, not just before or after lunch.

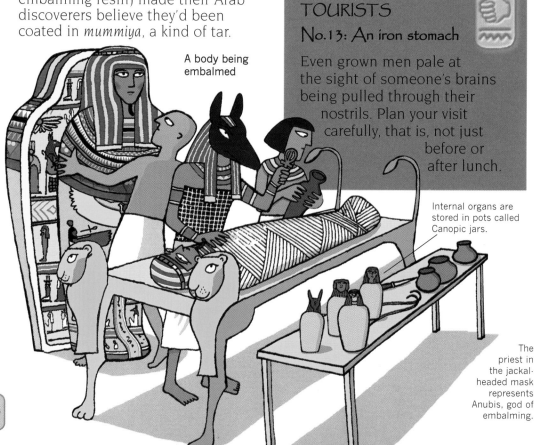

A body being embalmed

Internal organs are stored in pots called Canopic jars.

The priest in the jackal-headed mask represents Anubis, god of embalming.

A BEGINNER'S GUIDE...

Workers called *wetyw* (bandagers) first coat the head in resin to preserve it and remove the brain, which they throw away. The stomach, intestines, liver and lungs are removed through a cut on the left-hand side of the abdomen and mummified separately.

The heart is left intact, or replaced with a *scarab* (a charm of a sacred beetle) if it's accidentally damaged. The body is then rinsed, packed with stuffing and left in natron (a moisture-absorbing salt) for up to 40 days.

A finished mummy with a painted face

Mummies are wrapped in up to 20 layers of bandages, glued together with resin.

> 66 My corpse is permanent, it will not perish nor be destroyed in this land for ever. 99
>
> Spell 154, from the Book of the Dead

AFTER DRYING

A dried-out body won't be like any body you've seen. It's much darker, and weighs three-quarters less. Arms and legs are matchstick-thin and the skin is stiff and hangs in folds. At this point, the embalmer's skill comes into its own. The body is emptied, rinsed out and restuffed with resin-soaked linen or sawdust, herbs and spices. It's then massaged with oils to restore the skin's softness. The face is also made up, all to create as lifelike an appearance as possible.

FINISHING TOUCHES

A coat of resin is plastered on and the body is decked with jewels. Then it's wrapped in bandages and placed in the first of several linen shrouds, layered with amulets (charms) for luck. The final touch is a funeral mask over the head.

ANIMAL MUMMIES

Don't be surprised to see animals being embalmed, from cats and dogs to crocodiles; baboons to beetles. This isn't so Egyptians' pets can join them in the next world, but because certain animals are believed to be the animal form of a particular god or goddess. (They also make popular souvenirs.)

A mummified dog

DEATH ON THE NILE

Death may be an unusual subject for a vacation guide to dwell on, but you can't escape it in Ancient Egypt. It's not that the Egyptians are morbid – far from it. Attend one of their parties and you'll see they live life to the full. They just believe life on this earth is only the beginning. After death, comes a hazardous journey through Duat, the underworld, to the Field of Reeds in the Other World (heaven).

To ensure a body reaches the Other World intact, the mummy is placed in a protective, human-shaped coffin. Coffins are painted with decorative scenes and magic signs, to help the deceased on the journey to the Field of Reeds. Royalty, who always go several better, don't just have one wooden coffin. They get a whole nest of them – with the inner coffins made of solid gold – plus a sarcophagus (stone coffin) to boot.

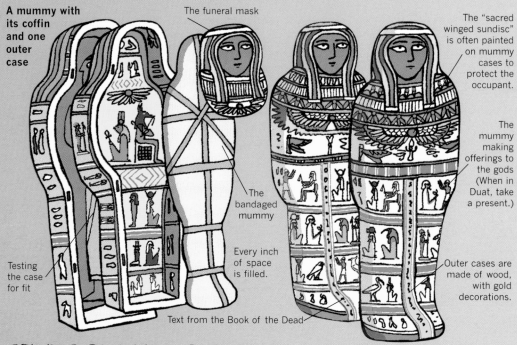

A mummy with its coffin and one outer case

The funeral mask

The "sacred winged sundisc" is often painted on mummy cases to protect the occupant.

The bandaged mummy

The mummy making offerings to the gods (When in Duat, take a present.)

Testing the case for fit

Every inch of space is filled.

Outer cases are made of wood, with gold decorations.

Text from the Book of the Dead

SPIRITS ON THE MOVE

Egyptians believe various spirits are born with a person, and that these have a life of their own after death. The three most important spirits are:

Ka: the life force – a person's physical double. The Ka can move around the tomb, so doors are painted on coffins to let it out.

Ba: a person's character; it roams the earth during the day but returns to the tomb at night.

Akh: a person's immortality; after death, it joins the stars.

Coffins have clear (if flattering) portraits of their occupants, so the Ba can find its body.

BOOK OF THE DEAD

Not content to rely on charms in bandages and symbols on coffins, spells are used to help the dead person pass through Duat safely. In pyramid times, these were carved on tomb walls. Now, the *Book of the Dead* (up to nearly 200 spells written on papyrus) is slipped in a coffin.

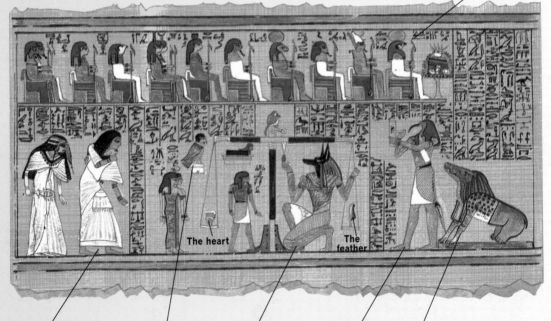

A scarab charm

Each version of the book is slightly different. The rich have their books custom-made, choosing the spells they think they'll need; poorer customers buy books already written, with a gap for their name.

WEIGHING THE HEART

A person has to undergo many trials before he can enter the Field of Reeds. One of the most famous spells in the *Book of the Dead* concerns the final trial: Weighing the Heart. Before a jury of 12, the heart is balanced against an ostrich feather, symbol of truth and justice.

If it's too full of wickedness, the heart will outweigh the feather and, in theory, the person is doomed. In practice, a scarab-shaped stone is often put into the body to make sure that, through magic, the person passes the test.

A scene from the Book of the Dead, showing the "Weighing the Heart" ceremony

Gods make up the jury.

The heart

The feather

The dead person is shown watching...

... his Ba hovering by the scales.

Anubis weighs the heart.

Thoth records the outcome.

Ammit, a monster, is given the heart if it fails the test.

A FUNERAL PROCESSION

With death rates high, if you spend any time at a major tomb site, you're bound to see a funeral. Even the wealthy, who can expect to live longest, rarely make it past their mid-fifties; many don't survive childhood. You may even see the funeral of a prince or princess, since the Pharaoh has dozens of wives and innumerable children.

THE FINAL JOURNEY

Funerals, for the rich at least, take place 70 days after death. On the day of the funeral, the mourners cross to the West Bank, collecting the mummy on their way to the tomb. Funerals are solemn, but there's nothing gloomy about them. You'll hear the procession long before you see it, the wailing of the professional mourners rising above a constant chanting of prayers.

The long walk to the tomb

Family and friends, priests and professional mourners follow the mummy to the tomb.

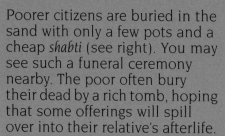
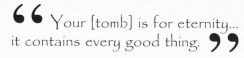

❝ Your [tomb] is for eternity... it contains every good thing. ❞

An inscription on a stela

Forget funerals back home: here, they are more like moving house. In effect, this is what the dead person is doing. Taking up most of the procession are servants laden with everything the mummy may need in the afterlife: furniture, chests of clothes and food, board games and even slippers.

OPEN WIDE

In the tomb, the chief priest performs a final rite: the Opening of the Mouth ceremony. This restores bodily functions to the mummy, so it can enjoy the afterlife. The priest touches the mummy with special instruments and recites spells. Some tombs contain statues as a spare home for the Ka (the life force spirit) in case anything happens to the mummy. King Khafre had 23 statues, all of which had to have their mouths opened.

A priest in animal skin heads the procession, burning incense.

Oxen drag a sled, which carries the boat-shaped bier (platform for a coffin) on which the mummy lies.

EAT, DRINK & BE MERRY

As well as religious paintings, tomb walls are covered with pictures of food to feed the Ka. In case that isn't enough to satisfy the spirit, fresh food and drink are left too. Tutankhamun was buried with over 100 baskets of fruit. Models of food are thought just as effective. Early Egyptians had entire model bakeries entombed with them.

SHABTIS

Even in paradise, crops have to be sown and canals dug. Initially, the dead were buried with models of their servants. Nowadays, *shabtis* (tiny models of mummies) are used. In years to come, Egyptians with money to burn will have up to 401 shabtis in their tombs: a servant for every day of the year and 36 overseers to keep the servants working.

A shabti (or mini-mummy)

> 66 O shabti, if the deceased is called upon to do any work [to cultivate the fields or irrigate the river banks] you shall say, "Here I am, I will do it." 99
>
> Spell 6, from the Book of the Dead, inscribed on shabtis

This model boat was left in an early tomb to ensure ample supplies of fish. (It won't work in an empty food cupboard.)

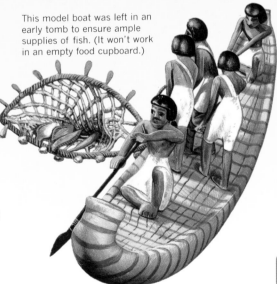

AN EXPEDITION TO NUBIA

On Egypt's southern border lies Nubia. Though less fertile than Egypt, Nubia is rich in natural resources, such as amethysts and gold. Nubia is also the corridor into central Africa with its wealth of ebony and ivory. If you can extend your trip to include a visit here, grab your chance.

Egypt

Africa

Egypt

Egypt and Africa

Nile

Egypt

Nile

Elephantine Island

Aswan

First Cataract

Nubia

Second Cataract

Under Egyptian control

Third Cataract

Fourth Cataract

Area of Egyptian influence

Nubia lies between the First and Second Cataracts (as shown on the larger map). A Cataract is where the path of the Nile is blocked by rocks.

CHIEF OF CHIEFS

The governor in overall charge of Nubia is called the *King's Son of Kush*. He's assisted by two deputies, one for the north, and one for the south. The region is divided into smaller areas, governed by local chiefs. You may be able to join the party of a new governor, going to Nubia to take up his post.

WAR & PEACE

The history of the Egyptians and Nubians is a troubled one. Eager to protect trade routes and exploit Nubia's resources, the Egyptians have been attacking Nubia since records began. For now, Egypt rules Nubia and there's peace. Egyptian towns and temples have sprung up, and the Nubians have adapted to their occupiers' way of life.

ISLAND HOPPING

On the way to Nubia, you'll pass several islands. The one to visit is **Elephantine Island**. On its south-east shore is a Nilometer: a long narrow staircase leading into the Nile. It was built to monitor the country's annual floods. Once officials know how high the Nile has flooded, they can decide whether it will be a good or bad year for crops and set the taxes accordingly.

Markings on the wall show how high the Nile is flooding.

RAINING GOLD

If you're lucky, you'll see the old governor being fêted at the famous Gold Ceremony. This takes place at the "Window of Appearances", a particular balcony on any one of Ramesses' many palaces. Gold collars are thrown down by the pharaoh to reward loyal and hard-working officials.

IVORY MARKET

An official party is bound to call at Elephantine Island, as it's the site of the main market for **Aswan**, a city near the Nubian border. The market is a useful port of call if you need to stock up on anything. Its main trade, though, was once in ivory, which may be how Elephantine Island got its name.

An ivory game piece from the First Dynasty

TOP TIPS FOR TOURISTS

No. 15: Split the cost

If there's an official trip to Nubia and money's tight, you could sign on as a deckhand for the voyage. (Get clearance from the guards first!) Or ask around to see if a minor official (such as a scribe) is willing to go halves on renting a boat. You can share the costs of the trip and camp on board.

NUBIAN MINES

Heating crushed rock to extract the gold

Workers blow on the fire to make it hotter.

Soldiers run and guard the camp.

A Nubian gold mine

Working at the rockface

Most of Egypt's gold comes from Nubia. As you sail upriver, you'll be near the sites of several gold and copper mines. If you're with a new governor, he's certain to stop off and journey into the desert to inspect them. Visiting a camp, you'll be glad you're only a tourist. Mining is back-breaking work and life is hard for the prisoners of war and criminals who work in the mines.

BUHEN FORT & THE ARMY

Visiting Nubia you're ideally placed to see an Egyptian fort. Around the Second Cataract is a string of nine, built in the Middle Kingdom to monitor traffic between Egypt and Nubia. Forts fall into two categories: "Plains" and "Cataract." Plains forts are much larger, generally rectangular, and built in open spaces. Cataract ones are smaller and irregular shapes (even triangular) to fit their environment.

BUHEN FORT

The Plains fort at **Buhen** is one of the most elaborate, with an outer wall of over 8 million bricks. It's more than 700m (2,310ft) long, 8m (26ft) high and 4m (13ft) thick. This surrounds an inner wall, which is even higher and thicker. Behind the walls lies an entire town, with barracks, officers' homes, granaries, storerooms, workshops and stables.

The town is laid out in a grid pattern. Paved streets run between the buildings connecting with a street which runs all the way around the inner wall.

WEAPONS

Soldiers have a wide range of weapons at their disposal, from bows and arrows, to swords, the recently introduced scimitars, axes and maces (clubs). In practice though, each unit tends to specialize in one, becoming master of the sword, say, rather than average with them all. Proficiency with weapons is essential: a soldier's only protection comes from his wooden shield, plus a padded jerkin, or leather bands fixed to his tunic, if he's lucky.

A scimitar

One of the great Nubian forts under attack by daring raiders

Battlements protect the soldiers, while holes in the walls let archers rain down arrows on the enemy.

SOLDIER SOLDIER

The current large professional army, vital to conquer an Empire, dates from only the last dynasty. Before that, the army was simply royal bodyguards, supported by trained peasants made to fight in a crisis. Now, soldiers from all classes volunteer. A career in the army offers wealth and adventure.

Soldiers are infantry (footsoldiers), or charioteers.

Charioteers come from the upper class (because of the cost of chariots and horses), but a poor family background won't prevent a boy from rising through the ranks.

Forts are sited on hills, where possible, to make life more difficult for the attackers.

CAMPAIGNS

A military expedition is an impressive sight. Added to the thousands of soldiers, there's quite an entourage of scouts, messengers, doctors, priests, cooks, grooms and servants, not forgetting the scribes who organize supplies and keep a daily record, and the hundreds of donkeys carrying bags and tents.

ARMY DIVISIONS

Heading the army is the pharaoh, who often accompanies his men on campaigns. Under him, generals and officers control the ranks. Men are grouped into **divisions** of 5,000, comprising 4,000 infantry and 500 two-man chariots. Each division, named after a god such as Amun or Re, has 20 **companies** of 200 infantrymen and 25 chariots. The infantry are sub-divided into **units** of 50 men. Each company has its own name and battle standard.

The upper walls have an overhang to allow soldiers to drop missiles on the attackers – if they dare leave their cover.

The enemy is ready to fire the second an Egyptian soldier pokes his head over the wall.

ABU SIMBEL

To Ramesses II, size is *everything*. Nowhere is this more apparent than at his massive temple at **Abu Simbel**. It was built to impress the Nubians with the pharaoh's power and dedicated to Amun-Re, the sun god Re-Harakhte and Ptah – plus Ramesses himself of course. With the entrance cut into a cliff-face, the body of the temple goes deep into the rock.

SEATED GUARDS

As you approach, you'll be greeted by four gigantic statues of Ramesses on his throne. At 20m (65ft) high, they really are colossal.

Hieroglyphs are painted all over the temple's facade.

Figures of Ramesses' family stand between the four statues, barely reaching their calves. Look out for the row of 22 stone baboons above the statues, beside a statue of Re-Harakhte (too small to see in the picture above). Baboons are thought wise because they seem to worship Re. Early Egyptians had noticed wild baboons racing up a cliff face at dawn and raising their paws to the sun. In fact, they were trying to warm themselves.

The statues are brightly painted, standing out against the desert rocks.

All four statues of Ramesses II wear the double crown of Upper and Lower Egypt.

The smaller statue on the left is of Nefertari, Ramesses' chief wife.

INSIDE THE TEMPLE

You're very unlikely to be allowed inside the temple (a right reserved for priests and the pharaoh alone) but if no one's looking you can peek through the doorway. Covering the walls are carvings of scenes from Ramesses' military victories. From the first hall, eight statues of Osiris lead to a hypostyle hall. Beyond this second hall, deep in the heart of the temple, lies the sanctuary, with seated statues of Ramesses, and the gods Amun-re, Re-Harakhte and Ptah.

Each vast statue of Osiris is a pillar 10m (32ft) high. Four statues stand on either side of the hallway.

All eight statues have Ramesses' face.

The door at the end leads to the sanctuary.

TOP TIPS FOR TOURISTS

No. 16: Re's rays

If you're here in October or February, try to visit the temple on the 20th. (You'll have to get up early, but it's worth it.) On those two days, just after dawn, the sun shines through the entrance and down the temple's entire length. For five minutes, the sanctuary statues at the far end are flooded with light.

QUEEN NEFERTARI'S TEMPLE

Beside the Great Temple is a smaller, simpler one, dedicated to Nefertari and the goddess Hathor.

That Ramesses should build a temple to one of his wives, even a chief one, is rare in itself. But statues of Nefertari also adorn the entrance, a privilege usually reserved for the king alone. It's certainly a more lasting token of affection than roses.

Remarkably, the statues of Nefertari are the same height as the four of husband Ramesses alongside.

SHOPPING

There are no shops as such, but every town or village you stop in will have a market. The choice of goods will depend on the size of the town and skills of its inhabitants. One town may have a good basket-maker, for instance, happy to trade a basket for a few beads. For top quality items, though, your best bet is a royal or temple workshop. Not surprisingly, the pharaoh keeps the best craftsmen for himself.

A typical market scene

Fruit, vegetables, bread and beer can be picked up daily.

Some craftsmen work from home, selling the finished products from their front yards.

SOUVENIRS

There's no shortage of unusual presents to take home. You could buy a pair of papyrus sandals to use as slippers. Mass-produced items include amulets and scarabs. Other easily portable items include cosmetics. At the other end of the scale, you could take back an inlaid wooden chest. An entire industry produces goods for the tomb, which anyone can buy. A shabti, complete with case, is an excellent souvenir.

FAÏENCE

Faïence (a type of glazed pottery) is used for everything from beads and vases to wall tiles. It's made by heating powdered quartz and always used to be bright blue. This is still its most common form, but faïence objects now also come in shades of yellow, red and green.

A faïence hedgehog – hedgehogs are thought to have magical powers of protection.

Examine expensive
items marked as "ebony" very
carefully. They may be made
of cheap wood, which has
simply been coated in thick
black varnish. Be wary of
painted items too. Paint is
sometimes used to disguise
a patchwork job, where
several different woods have
been used in one piece.

GLASSWARE

Glass-making is a relatively recent
invention and you'll find amazingly
decorated vases and dishes. Stripes
are a common theme, made by
winding threads of glass around
a dish or vase and heating them
until they merge in.

This open-mouthed
glass fish is a
container for
perfume oil.

POTTERY & STONE

Pots are made of clay and finely
chopped straw, mixed by
being trampled underfoot.
Potters have wheels, but
they are operated by
hand. If the potter has
no assistant to turn the
wheel, he has to make
his pots one-handed.
The pots are then
baked in a wood-
burning kiln.

Recently, there's
been a craze for
painted pots.
Stone is also
used for pots and
vases: limestone
for household
goods; alabaster
for luxury items.

A gold lion's-head
necklace from the expensive
end of the market

COSTUME JEWELS

Everyone here wears jewels to liven
up an otherwise basic wardrobe.
The choice ranges from a simple
"lucky charm" necklace (three
beads on a leather string), to an
elaborate neck collar strung with
thousands of beads.

If you're short of things to barter,
go for less expensive copper items.
But if money's no object, the gold
and silver trinkets on offer will
astound you. Stone beads also
make necklaces pricey, as they're
drilled by hand (which takes time).
Cheaper by far are faïence beads.

ENTERTAINMENT

When it comes to entertainment, don't expect it laid out on a plate. There are no plays in Egypt, unless you count the performances put on by temples, dramatizing the lives of the gods. In fact, the only public spectacles (though well worth seeing) are religious festivals and royal processions. So, on the whole, people tend to make their own fun.

PARTIES

All Egyptians love parties and the wealthy entertain on a grand scale. If you're invited to a banquet, it will be lavish. The food and drink will flow all night and you'll be entertained by jugglers, dancers, acrobats, wrestlers and story-tellers. You won't need to lift a finger either. Servants bring all the refreshments to you.

❝ I have heard that you have abandoned writing and that you whirl around in pleasures. . . **❞**

Teacher to a
partying pupil

A pair of clappers
used like castanets

MUSIC

You'll hear a wide range of instruments (not to mention musicians). The oldest instrument is the reed or wooden flute, but bands also have oboes, lutes, or lyres, with drums and clappers (shown left) for rhythm. As the evening wears on, a harpist may accompany a story-teller.

DANCING

Even if the music has a lively beat, dancing is strictly a spectator sport. Routines are performed by professionals only. If you want to dance, you'll have to visit one of the seedier taverns. Here you can dance to your heart's content – but you'll take your life in your hands. You also risk arrest. Taverns are rowdy and frequently raided by the police.

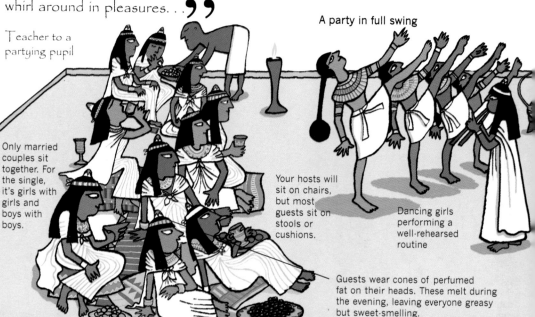

A party in full swing

Only married couples sit together. For the single, it's girls with girls and boys with boys.

Your hosts will sit on chairs, but most guests sit on stools or cushions.

Dancing girls performing a well-rehearsed routine

Guests wear cones of perfumed fat on their heads. These melt during the evening, leaving everyone greasy but sweet-smelling.

TOYS & GAMES

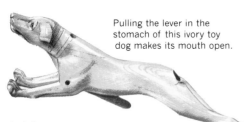

Pulling the lever in the stomach of this ivory toy dog makes its mouth open.

Children grow up quickly, learning adult responsibilities from an early age. Toys, like the wooden dog above, painted dolls and balls, are soon left behind. Games, however, continue into adulthood, with board games called *Senet* and *Hounds and Jackals* being especially popular.

TOP TIPS FOR TOURISTS

No. 18: A quick dip

There are no swimming pools, but the Nile is clean to swim in. A word of warning: if you try it, look out for crocodiles.

SPORTS

Hunting and fishing are enjoyed by all sections of male society. Other sports, also for men only, include archery, wrestling, boxing and fencing with sticks. Men also enjoy swimming, as do women. (It's one of the few sports they can take part in.)

RIVER OUTINGS

Outside the home, most fun is to be had on the river. You can take out a boat, picnic on the river bank, or watch a boating contest. In a typical match, two teams, standing up in boats, try to knock each other into the river using long wooden poles.

Servants bring around water bowls, so you can rinse your fingers after the stickier courses.

A harpist and lute player accompany the dancers.

Faïence dishes piled high with dates for guests with a sweet tooth

Chatting about a forthcoming trip on the Nile

45

HUNTING & WILDLIFE

The Egyptians have two distinct views on nature. On the one hand, they certainly appreciate its beauty. You only have to study their paintings to see that. But they're also practical, convinced that nature exists for their personal use, whether food or sport. Don't feel you have to adopt local customs. You can enjoy the wildlife in its natural habitat without harming a hair.

HUNTING

Hunting is said to be the sport of kings, and pharaohs are no exception. Out in the desert, Ramesses and his nobles trap lions or antelopes in nets, and then let fly with arrows from the safety of their chariots. Professional huntsmen and dogs help drive the animals beforehand, so it's not so much hunting as target practice.

A bull trapped in a makeshift pen

TOP TIPS FOR TOURISTS

No. 19: Watch out!

If you go on a desert hunt, be careful not to get in the way of the nobles in their chariots. Horses and chariots are very expensive. Any noble will put his team and chariot's safety above yours.

FOWLING

Fowling, or catching birds, is a living for peasants, who trap marsh birds in vast nets. Nobles, with the leisure to miss, toss a *throw-stick* (a curved piece of wood) at birds individually, hoping to break their necks.

If you hurl a throw-stick into a papyrus thicket, watch your aim. The first throw tells the birds you're there and they'll fly.

These two hunters aren't so much brave as foolhardy. Hunting a hippo usually takes a team of men.

A HIPPO HUNT

Lurking in the Nile are hippos and crocodiles and both are targeted by huntsmen. A hippo surfacing under a reed boat is certain disaster. But hippos aren't only killed because of the nuisance factor. A hippo hunt is dangerous – the ideal way for men to show off their courage and skill. There's also a religious side. The hippo is one of the forms taken by the evil god Set. The king is often shown harpooning a hippo, to symbolize the destruction of evil.

A model hippo made of faience

FISHING

You'll meet two types of fishermen on the river. Nobles hunt for fun, fishing with baited hooks or using harpoons to spear fish as they swim by. Peasants, who fish to earn their living, work in teams and drag a net between two boats.

PETS

The Egyptians don't just think of animals as food or sport. Dogs are very popular as pets, short-legged lap dogs especially. Cats are now common too, though they were only adopted as pets in the Middle Kingdom. Other pets are monkeys, geese, and even gazelles.

Ramesses has a pet lion, "Tearer to pieces of his enemies", who roars into action alongside his chariot in war. You may spot "Tearer" in a procession, trotting beside the king. Ramesses also has a soft spot for two horses that saved his life in battle.

> 66 [It's] a happy day when we go down to the marsh... [to] ...snare birds and catch many fishes in the... waters. 99
>
> Taken from *The Pleasures of Fishing and Fowling*, an early manuscript

Fowling and fishing on the Nile

These days, only hunters use reed boats such as those shown here. Most other boats are made of wood.

A team of peasants checking the day's catch

Harpooning a fish rather than using a net needs quick reflexes.

FARMING

CROPS

Considering the vast amounts of bread and beer Egyptians consume, it's no surprise that the main crops are wheat (a type called emmer), and barley. Other crops grown include a wide variety of fruit and vegetables. Some farmers grow flax, too, which is made into linen and used for clothes. Young flax plants make fine thread; older ones provide a thicker thread, for heavy fabric, ropes and matting.

Leeks, onions, garlic and peas

Pomegranate, grapes and figs

WINE PRODUCTION

Grapes are eaten off the vine and also used for wine. They're hand-picked, pressed twice to extract the juice, left in open jars to ferment, then poured into new jars and sealed.

Grapes are crushed by foot in a grape press. The juice is collected in a large tub, or vat.

TILLING & SOWING

Wooden frames with bronze blades attached are used to till (turn over) the land before crops are sown. If the earth is too hard for lightweight blades, a hoe is used first. (Spades and shovels are unheard of.) Whatever the crop, animals are driven behind the sower, to ensure the seeds are well trodden in.

Tilling and sowing often take place together.

WATERING THE LAND

Since there's no rain, a network of canals was built centuries ago to store floodwater. The canals carry the water from the Nile to the fields via a series of connecting channels and ditches.

By alternately blocking and reopening channels, farmers can control the flow of water to their crops. To get the water from ditch to field, however, needs a strong fieldworker. A recent invention, the *shaduf* (shown below, to the left), makes life easier.

A *shaduf* is a bucket fixed to a counterweight and balanced on a beam. It may not seem hi-tech to you, but try lifting the bucket without it.

THE TAXMAN COMETH

Though everyone wants a good crop, it heralds the arrival of an unwelcome visitor: the taxman. Along with a team of civil servants, the taxman measures the growing crops, to assess how much will be harvested – and how much the pharaoh can cream off in taxes. A smart farmer has "gifts" on hand to help the taxman make this decision.

A taxman and civil servant measuring the crops while the farmer and his wife look on

Having to pay a percentage of his profit to the king, a farmer accepts with a resigned shrug. The problem arises when, whatever his eventual harvest, the original assessment stands. So, even if a sudden plague of locusts wipes out an entire crop, the pharaoh expects the same taxes as if the abundant crop forecast had materialized.

THE HARVEST

Probably, your only contact with the harvest, which falls in March and April, will be the easiest part of all: one of the numerous festivals to celebrate its end. For farmers, this is the culmination of several months of backbreaking work. The harvest itself has three stages:

Cutting: First, men cut the ears of grain with sickles. The grain is then carried away in baskets slung on poles or donkeys. Any left behind is gleaned (picked up) by women and children following close on the harvesters' heels.

Threshing: This is the second stage, where the grain is separated from the chaff (husks). The grain is scattered upon an area known as the threshing floor and roughly forked over, before cattle are let loose to trample upon it.

Winnowing: Finally, the flattened ears are scooped up by female workers and tossed into the air, a process called winnowing. The light chaff floats away, leaving the grain. This is stored in granaries, the amount carefully recorded by a scribe before the king's cut is carted off.

If you visit at harvest time, you'll see winnowing women.

ANNUAL CYCLE

Once all is safely gathered in, irrigation ditches must be repaired and new channels dug, ready for the floods in July. After that, farming halts until October, when farmers repair any flood damage and check that the boundary stones marking their fields are still in place.

RELIGION & FESTIVALS

RELIGION

For Egyptians, religion is so bound up with everyday life it's inseparable from it. Gods aren't remote deities. They live among them – if only in spirit form – hidden in temples.

Egyptian beliefs arose as an attempt to explain the mysteries of the world, though explanations can vary, depending on where in Egypt you are. To make things more complicated, over the last 2,000 years, as new beliefs have developed, old ideas have simply been tagged on to them.

One of the most common themes is the balance of order against chaos. This "order" is maintained by temple rituals, living a decent life and the king ruling with justice.

THE PEOPLE'S RELIGION

Since few people may go beyond temple courtyards (and most can't get that far), small shrines have been set up where locals can pray to the gods and leave offerings. Rooms in Egyptian homes have niches where statues of gods are kept. Many people also carry amulets with charms to ward off evil spirits. It's at this point religion and magic become blurred. The Egyptians are strong believers in the power contained in objects. Don't offend anyone or they may attack an effigy (model) of you.

The theories of creation

Re created all things. One theory says he emerged from a sacred lotus flower.

Some say Re was hatched from an egg laid by the Great Cackler, a goose.

Others think Re first appeared as a scarab beetle.

TEMPLES & PRIESTS

There's no organized religion as such. Temples aren't places of worship; they're where the gods live. Priests don't preach; they are live-in servants, feeding and entertaining the gods three times a day. Egyptians feel an overwhelming gratitude for all the gods have given them. It's only fair, runs the argument, that the gods get the best of everything in return. Any food the gods don't eat is passed on to temple workers as wages. Temples are the largest employers in Egypt. Karnak alone has over 81,000 on the payroll.

PURE IN BODY

To an Egyptian, cleanliness isn't next to godliness, it *is* godliness. Demons are said to live in dirt and priests wash seven times and chew natron (a salt) to cleanse themselves, every time they enter a temple. They only wear white linen, which is frequently washed. On top of that, they shave all over every other day.

Near a temple, don't be surprised if someone wafts an incense burner up your tunic. He's simply trying to smoke out demons.

FESTIVALS

Festivals are a chance for Egyptians to interact more closely with their gods, since on these occasions the statues are brought out from the shrines. The first one described below ensures the well-being of the king. If he stays well, says the theory, so will Egypt.

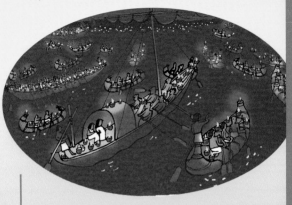

Boats cross the Nile in the early morning for the **Feast of the Valley**. The Nile is ablaze with candles and torches.

Sed (Jubilee): an ancient custom, celebrated on the 30th anniversary of a king's reign and periodically after that. The king runs between two markers to prove his fitness to rule and renew his strength.

The king running for Sed: today the run is symbolic.

Opet: a more recent festival, held at the start of the year. The barques (sacred boats) of the god Amun, his wife Mut and son Khonsu are carried in procession from the temple at Karnak to Luxor, about 3km (almost a couple of miles) away.

Feast of the Valley: this may be a festival for the dead but it's a lively affair. The statue of Amun is taken from its shrine at Karnak and ferried over to the tombs on the West Bank.

If you don't mind heights, arrive early and climb the West Bank cliffs. There's a competition to see who can be the first to spot the glint of gold that indicates Amun's statue has left the temple. Tombs are lit by lamplight and families hold banquets for their dead relatives.

Mystery Plays: for a little drama, visit Abydos to see a masked play about Osiris and Set (see page 28). You could join in but be prepared for it to degenerate into a brawl. Religion is taken seriously over here. Egyptians support their chosen gods with all the enthusiasm of football fans.

Priests acting out a mystery play

CLOTHES & FASHION

WHAT'S HOT

Little changed in fashion for 1,500 years. What was worn in the First Dynasty was still trendy throughout the Middle Kingdom. But, as the New Kingdom continues, suddenly fashion itself is all the rage. Clothes are looser, more flowing and far more elaborate, and pleats are very much in.

Noblemen wear a kilt (wraparound skirt) topped by layers of fine pleated robes tied at the waist with a sash. Upper class women wear fine dresses, topped with a shawl made from one piece of cloth.

A loose, thin cloak for men is very fashionable.

Dresses and tunics for the lower classes are simpler and made from coarser cloth. Linen is the main fabric (often white, as that's thought pure) and used for almost everything – although winter wraps and cloaks are sometimes made from wool.

Noblewomen's shawls are folded around the body and knotted on the chest.

WHAT'S NOT

Until recently, most men wore only a short linen kilt. Women had an equally simple sheath dress to the ankles, held up by shoulder straps. Children wore kilts too, though in summer they usually ran around naked. Officials and noblemen wore longer, pleated kilts, while noblewomen's dresses were patterned and dyed different shades.

An elaborate Middle Kingdom party frock, covered with beads.

HAIR & WIGS

Most people shave their heads to keep cool and then wear a fancy wig made from human or artificial hair. During the Middle Kingdom, padded and decorated hair was in vogue for a while. Men now keep their hair shortish. The trend for women was long and straight, but masses of braids and curls are now in. Children have shaved heads (to prevent lice) but keep enough hair for a braid: "the sidelock of youth". In paintings, a subject shown with no clothes and a shaved head is a child.

Woman

New Kingdom hairstyles à la mode

Man

A boy's sidelock (girls' braids are longer)

SHOES

Everyone goes barefoot for much of the time. For occasions when you need to be more formal, slip on sandals made from papyrus reeds or leather. The upper classes tend to go in for highly decorated footwear. Tutankhamun had a snazzy pair of gold embossed sandals for special occasions.

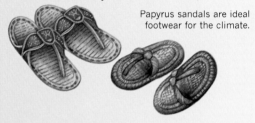

Papyrus sandals are ideal footwear for the climate.

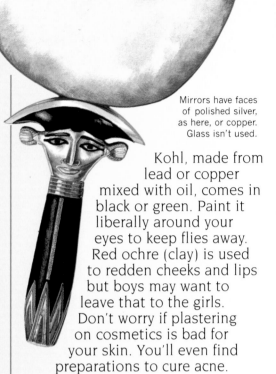

Mirrors have faces of polished silver, as here, or copper. Glass isn't used.

Kohl, made from lead or copper mixed with oil, comes in black or green. Paint it liberally around your eyes to keep flies away. Red ochre (clay) is used to redden cheeks and lips but boys may want to leave that to the girls. Don't worry if plastering on cosmetics is bad for your skin. You'll even find preparations to cure acne.

TOILETRIES

It's not just priests who keep clean. Everyone washes, either in the river or with a jug and basin, if not a shower, at home. There's no soap, but you'll find a cleansing cream made from oil, lime and perfume readily available. As for shampoo – there are mixtures to cure dandruff and baldness. Tempted to change your hair shade? You can buy henna shampoo and dye your hair red.

COSMETICS

Both sexes wear cosmetics and perfumed oils, partly as a fashion statement

A box for eyepaint

but mostly as protection against the fierce Egyptian sun. You should rub in oils daily to prevent your skin from cracking and drying out. Stock up on kohl eyepaint too.

ACCESSORIES

Jewels are worn by everyone from the pharaoh to the poorest peasant, to decorate fairly basic clothing. If bracelets and rings aren't your thing, try a pectoral (fancy pendant hung around the neck) or an ever-popular bead collar. Important men also carry a staff to show off their social standing.

A pectoral and the latest fashion item: big earrings

EDUCATION

THE WRITE THING

When you consider that the majority of the population can't read and write, it's hardly surprising that those who can are highly thought of. Scribes, who write and copy texts and keep records, enjoy great privileges, prestige and power. For some, it's the first step up the ladder of government service.

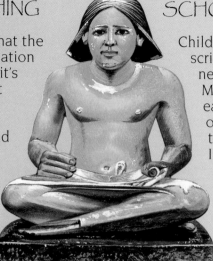

A statue of a scribe

SCHOOL OF KNOCKS

Children are taught by scribes, who aren't necessarily good teachers. Many believe, "a boy's ears are on his back." In other words, to get him to listen, beat him. Insults, such as, "You... are thicker than a tall obelisk..." are par for the course. No one's beaten for talking though. Even scribes read words aloud before they copy them down.

SCHOOLS

Public schools, attached to temples, government offices and the palace, are for the sons of scribes and the higher classes only. Most boys from poorer families learn their fathers' trades; girls help their mothers at home. A few villages have schools run by local priests or scribes, though they charge. Even so, many peasants struggle to scrape the fees together. Some nobles prefer to educate their sons at home, hiring a private tutor. Daughters are often included in these lessons.

LESSONS

Boys start their first school at seven. Perhaps because scribes are not formally trained as teachers, lessons are uninspired. There's no alphabet, so pupils spend hours memorizing characters and phrases for the Egyptian scripts (see pages 56-57).

The rest of the day is spent learning parrot-fashion, or copying classic works, such as "The Wisdom Texts" which lay down rules for how to behave. It's hoped that boys will absorb the advice while copying.

Egyptian boys from noble families writing down an ancient story their teacher is dictating

SECONDARY SCHOOL

Pupils go on to higher education at nine or ten. At this stage, they learn how to compose letters and legal documents, studying a range of subjects. Along with geography, history, languages and literature, religion and mathematics, boys are taught engineering, surveying, account-keeping, astronomy and medicine.

An astronomer's star chart showing the constellations in the form of gods

Students from wealthy families then specialize in only one or two subjects, such as engineering or languages, and enter government service. But most of the students go on to become scribes of some sort.

WRITING KIT

Young boys write on pieces of pottery or limestone flakes (known in modern times as *ostraca*), or wooden tablets covered with plaster.

A piece of *ostracon** which tells a popular tale

The tablets can be washed and used again, in much the same way as a blackboard.

*Ostracon is the singular of *ostraca*

PEN AND PAPER

Once they can write fluently, boys move on to writing on sheets of papyrus, a paper made from papyrus reeds. They write using reed pens and black, red or green ink made from mineral pigments. Ink comes in solid blocks and has to be mixed with water on a palette before it can be used, like paint.

Papyrus is the closest thing the Egyptians have to paper. Bear in mind that it varies in quality. If you're thinking of buying any, the best comes from the middle of the papyrus pith. It goes through several stages before you can write on it. Even then, it feels more like fabric than paper.

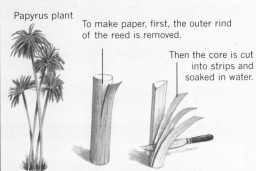

Papyrus plant

To make paper, first, the outer rind of the reed is removed.

Then the core is cut into strips and soaked in water.

Two layers of strips are pressed together at right angles. Starch in the core acts like glue. The sheet is beaten with a mallet and left to dry.

Finally, it is polished with a stone. Lots of sheets are joined together to form a scroll.

WRITE LIKE AN EGYPTIAN

HIEROGLYPHS

The Egyptians write using symbols known in modern times as *hieroglyphs*. As there are over 700 of them, you're unlikely to learn them all on one visit. You may start to recognize the more common ones, though, and you can always use this page as a handy reference.

Hieroglyphs take the form of pictures, but they're not simply picture writing. Originally, they just stood for the object they show but now they stand for sounds too.

A picture of an owl stands for the sound of an "m"

The hieroglyphs above are in an oval frame called a cartouche. They show the name Tutankhamun took on becoming king: Neb-kheperu-re.

Words are made up of several different symbols. An extra picture, called a determinative, is often placed at the end of a word, so there's no doubt about its meaning.

For example:

The sounds of "m", "j" and "w" make up the word "cat" but the sign has a cat on the end, too, to make it clear.

m   j   w

NO A, E, I, O, U...

There are no hieroglyphs for vowels. (It's only in the 19th century AD, when texts are translated, that scholars will give vowel sounds to some symbols, to make them easier to read.) The Egyptians don't worry about spelling either. They're far more concerned that a word looks right.

The word for beautiful, "nfr", is not written in a line, as above, but to fit a neat rectangle:

THE POWER OF THE PEN

"Hieroglyph" is a Greek word meaning "holy writing" but the Egyptians think of hieroglyphs as the "words of the gods."

Papyrus, reed pens and an ink block

They believe words have magical powers, creating the objects they describe – which is why hieroglyphs cover their temples and tombs.

READING ORDER

Hieroglyphs can be read from right to left, left to right or straight down. The way they're set out gives you the clue. If the people and animals in the pictures are facing left, you start from the left. If they face right, you read from right to left.

Read from left to right

Read from right to left

This column of hieroglyphs should be read from right to left and down.

Hieroglyphs you read down are often used on pillars or columns. Look out for them on the temples at Thebes.

Pharaohs' names are easy to spot as they are always shown in cartouches.

SHORTHAND

Hieroglyphs are always used on monuments but, for everyday use, two shorthand scripts called "Hieratic" and "Demotic" have been developed. These simplify the pictures and look more like handwriting.

Hieratic   **Demotic**

AN "ALPHABET"

(a)* = (vulture)

b = (leg)

d = (hand)

y (e) = (reed)

f (v) = (viper)

g = (stand for a jar)

q = (a slope)

r = (mouth)

s (c) = (folded cloth)

t = (loaf of bread)

h = (house with courtyard)

j = (cobra)

k = (basket)

m = (owl)

n = (water)

p = (wicker stool)

w = (quail)

y (i) = (double reed)

s (z) = (door bolt)

This alphabet has been invented for modern readers: the Egyptians don't have one.

* The letters in brackets are modern sounds.

GOVERNMENT & LAW

A PYRAMID SOCIETY

At the top of society is the pharaoh, the absolute ruler. Despite having absolute power, the pharaoh has no easy life (though admittedly, he has it easier than most). The king is expected to maintain the balance of the entire universe. He's responsible for the weather and harvest. He's a go-between for the gods and his people, and if Egypt goes to war, he must lead the army into battle.

Though the pharaoh has the final say, the day-to-day running of Egypt is in the hands of government departments. These include the Treasury, Royal Works (temples and tombs), the Granaries, Cattle and Foreign Affairs.

After the pharaoh, the two most important men are the viziers, one each in charge of Upper and Lower Egypt.

A pyramid of people showing the structure of Egyptian society

GOING DOWN

Under the viziers, mayors and governors run the towns and country districts. All have a staff of officials to collect taxes and carry out the orders of government departments. Lower down the pyramid come soldiers, craftsmen and farmers, followed by peasants and servants, with slaves at the bottom of the lot.

CLASS SNOBBERY

Even within classes, there's a definite order. Take scribes, for example. At the lowest level are clerks and letter-writers. One step up are community scribes and business secretaries. Nearer the top are local or regional officials, or scribes who administer an estate or temple. At the very top are the highest-ranking government officials.

Pharaoh

Viziers

Government ministers and high priests

Scribes belonging to many ranks

Town mayors, district governors, priests and doctors

Soldiers

Craftsman

Farmers and townspeople

Peasants

Slaves

TAXES

There are numerous taxes, paid with either produce or work. You should escape these though. There's no tax on tourists. Among the taxes are:

Tributes from conquered people in places such as Syria,

Land tax paid by farmers in grain, based on an estimated crop,

Craft tax paid by craftsmen on the goods they produce,

Hunting and fishing tax paid on all fish and game sold,

Import/export tax paid by traders.

A glassblower might pay his taxes in jugs

CORVÉE DUTY

Corvée is a tax paid for in work and everyone but the ruling classes is forced to undertake it. Officially, no one is exempt. In practice, the rich often pay poorer citizens to do their corvée for them. Corvée helps to ensure that vital jobs, such as irrigation repairs, are carried out. When the ground is too flooded to work on, farmers are sent to help out on the latest building project or down a quarry or mine.

WOMEN IN EGYPT

Women have a better time of it in Egypt than in many ancient cultures, with much personal freedom and the same legal duties and rights as men. A wife keeps her own property after divorce and a girl may inherit her father's estate – though this is more likely if she has no brothers.

JOBS FOR THE GIRLS

Though they are expected to marry young and raise a family, some women have a career outside the home. They can run businesses or farms (paying taxes), or become maids to noblewomen, gaining influence in important households. Temples take on female dancers, musicians and singers, and noblewomen can become courtiers or priestesses. Jobs for lower class girls include weaving, perfume-making and professional mourning.

Any girl can become a dancer – if she's fit enough. Some of the routines are very demanding.

LAW AND ORDER

There are laws on every aspect of life, upheld by the Medjay and, in a dispute, a *kenbet* (town court). All Egyptians, however poor, can have their day in court, as they represent themselves. They're always suing each other, so you may be called as a witness. Judges are local officials, who have been known to seek signs from the gods, if they can't decide on a verdict. In criminal cases, the accused is innocent until proven guilty, but anyone found guilty is suitably punished.

WHO'S WHO & DEFINITIONS

A "Who's who" of Ancient Egypt is largely made up of pharaohs, since they are by far the most important people in the country. As there are over 300 rulers, however, only a few are listed here. The dates of their reigns are shown in brackets.

Ahmes Nefertari (Dynasty XVIII): sister-wife of **Ahmose** and Queen of Egypt, she ruled on behalf of her son Amenhotep I until he was old enough to rule in his own right. They founded the community for royal tomb-builders (see page 25).

Ahmose (c.1552-1527BC Dynasty XVIII): the first king of the New Kingdom, he came to the throne as a child. In later years, he freed Egypt from the Hyksos, a people from the east who invaded and occupied Egypt between the Middle and New Kingdoms.

Akhenaten (c.1364-1347BC Dynasty XVIII): the king previously known as **Amenhotep IV**, he elevated the sun god Aten above all others, renaming himself and building a new capital, Akhetaten (modern Amarna). After his death, Egypt reverted to a multi-deity nation, his capital was abandoned and all of his monuments were destroyed.

Akhenaten

Amenhotep IV (see **Akhenaten**)

Djoser (c.2630-2611BC Dynasty III): king of Egypt, notable for having the first pyramid at Sakkara.

Hatshepsut (c.1490-1468BC Dynasty XVIII): appointed to rule on behalf of her young nephew, **Tuthmosis III**, she seized power and reigned as "king" for over 20 years. You won't see much evidence of her reign. Tuthmosis destroyed most of it.

A stone carving of **Hatshepsut**

Imhotep (Dynasty III): an official during **Djoser's** reign, he was the architect who designed the first step pyramid. Also a doctor and high priest, he's worshipped as a god in the New Kingdom.

Khufu/Cheops (c.2551-2528BC Dynasty IV): son of Sneferu, his pyramid, the Great Pyramid at Gizah, was the largest ever built.

Menes (c.3100BC): king of Upper Egypt, he conquered Lower Egypt, uniting the two kingdoms to become king of the First Dynasty.

Nefertari (Dynasty XIX): chief queen of **Ramesses II**, one of the temples at Abu Simbel was built for her. She also has a spectacular tomb in the Valley of the Queens.

Nefertiti (Dynasty XVIII): queen of Egypt and wife of **Akhenaten**, she was renowned for her beauty.

A painted stone bust of **Nefertiti**

Pepi II (c.2246-2152BC Dynasty VI): the last king of the Old Kingdom, he reigned for 94 years – the longest recorded reign in history.

Ramesses I (c.1305-1303BC Dynasty XIX): grandfather of **Ramesses II**, a former army officer and vizier to Horemheb, the last pharaoh of Dynasty XVIII. When Horemheb died without a son, Ramesses took the throne and founded Dynasty XIX.

Ramesses II (c.1289-1224BC Dynasty XIX): one of the most famous kings in Egyptian history, due in no small part to his gift for self-publicity. In the early part of his reign he fought the Hittites, who were building an empire in Asia Minor.

Ramesses II

Seti I (c.1303-1289BC Dynasty XIX): **Ramesses I**'s son. Seti had his own son, **Ramesses II**, crowned during his own lifetime, to ensure a peaceful succession.

Tutankhamun (c.1347-1337BC Dynasty XVIII): son of **Akhenaten**, he'll find fame in the 20th century when his tomb is discovered by Howard Carter, an archaeologist.

Tuthmosis III (c.1492-1436BC Dynasty XVIII): nephew of **Hatshepsut** and one of Egypt's greatest warriors.

One of **Tutankhamun**'s magnificent coffins

DEFINITIONS

amulet: a lucky charm
Cataract: a place where large rocks block the path of the Nile
Duat: the Underworld, where Egyptians go when they die, ruled over by the god Osiris, king of the dead
dynasty: a succession of rulers, often coming from the same family
embalming: the drying out of a body to preserve it after death
faïence: a type of glazed pottery
hieroglyphics: Egyptian writing, which uses pictures and symbols (hieroglyphs) to represent objects and sounds
ma'at: the balance of the universe
Medjay: the Egyptian police force
mummy: an **embalmed** body
necropolis: a cemetery
obelisk: a tall square column with a pointed top
ostracon (plural *ostraca*): broken pottery or stone which is written on
papyrus: a reed; also the name for a form of paper made from papyrus reed
pharaoh: king of Egypt
scribe: someone employed to write and copy texts and keep records
shrine: a small temple where a god or goddess is worshipped, or a container for a god's statue
shroud: a piece of cloth used to wrap a dead body
stela (plural *stelae*): a stone carved with inscriptions which are often prayers
succession: when a new ruler takes over
vizier: the pharaoh's chief minister

Amulets

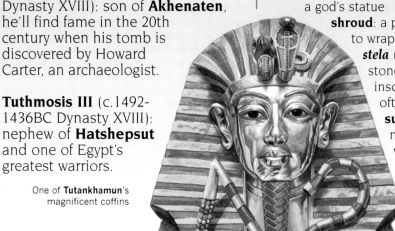

A TIMELINE OF DYNASTIES

Archaic Period c.3100-2649BC

Dynasty I
c.3100BC **Menes** unites Upper and Lower Egypt and builds a capital at Memphis
Kings are buried in mud-brick tombs

Dynasty II

Old Kingdom c.2649-2150BC
The pyramids are built

Dynasty III c.2649-2575BC Age of the step pyramids
Architect **Imhotep** builds the first step pyramid, for king **Djoser**

Dynasty IV c.2575-2467BC
c.2575-2551BC Reign of **Sneferu** who builds the first straight-sided pyramid
c.2551-2528BC Reign of **Khufu (Cheops)** during which his Great Pyramid is built at Gizah
c.2520-2494BC Khafre (Chephren)
c.2490-2472BC Menkaure (Mycerinus)

Dynasty V c.2467-2323BC

Dynasty VI c.2323-2150BC

2nd Intermediate Period c.1640-1552BC

Dynasties XV & XVI
The reign of the Hyksos kings in the north

Dynasty XVII c.1640-1552BC
The reign of Theban kings

New Kingdom c.1552-1069BC
The greatest period of the Egyptian empire
Royal tombs are built in the Valley of the Kings

Dynasty XVIII c.1552-1305BC
c.1552-1527BC Reign of **Ahmose**, conqueror of the Hyksos
c.1490-1468BC Reign of **Hatshepsut**, a queen who rules as a king
c.1490-1436BC Reign of **Tuthmosis III**, the greatest of the so-called "warrior pharaohs"
c.1364-1347BC Reign of **Akhenaten**
c.1347-1337BC Reign of **Tutankhamun**, the "boy-king"

Dynasty XIX c.1305-1186BC
c.1305-1303BC Reign of **Ramesses I**
c.1289-1224BC Reign of **Ramesses II**, a great warrior and prolific builder, whose rule lasts for nearly 70 years

Dynasty XX c.1186-1069BC The reign of nine more Ramesses (and a Set-nakht)

Names in **bold** are referred to on pages 60-61.
The pharaohs shown are those mentioned elsewhere in the guide.

1st Intermediate Period c.2150-2040BC

Dynasties VII & VIII
(short reigns of many kings)

Dynasties IX & X c.2134-2040BC
A new line of kings rules from Herakleopolis

Middle Kingdom c.2040-1640BC

Dynasty XI c.2040-1991BC Egypt is re-unified by a prince of Thebes
Thebes becomes the capital

Dynasty XII c.1991-1783BC Period of great cultural achievement
Nubia is conquered and forts are built

Dynasty XIII c.1783-1640BC
The short reigns of about 70 kings

Dynasty XIV c.1783-1640BC The reign of rebel princes who rule at the same time as Dynasty XIII
c.1674BC The Nile Delta is overrun with Hyksos, a people from the Middle East

3rd Intermediate Period
c.1069-663BC *During the later part of this period, several lines of kings rule simultaneously*

Dynasty XXI c.1069-945BC

Dynasty XXII c.945-715BC

Dynasty XXIII A separate line of kings who rule at the same time as the later kings from Dynasty XXII and Dynasty XXIV

Dynasty XXIV c.727-715BC Two pharaohs who rule at the same time as Dynasties XXII and XXIII

Dynasty XXV c.728-663BC
The rule of kings from Nubia Dynasty XXV overlaps with the start of Dynasty XXVI

Late Period 664-332BC
The Egyptians regain their independence from Nubia in 664BC

Dynasty XXVI 664-525BC

Dynasty XXVII 525-404BC The reign of kings from Persia, including one Cambyses (525-521BC) who lost his entire army in the Egyptian desert

Dynasties XXVIII - XXX 404-343BC
Egyptian princes overthrow the Persians and rule Egypt
343-342BC The Persians retake Egypt
Dynasty XXXI 341-332BC
The second reign of Persian kings

INDEX

Pharaohs, queens, gods and goddesses are listed in **bold**.
Numbers in **bold** refer to maps.